ROSES *of* CRIMSON FIRE

ROSES *of* CRIMSON FIRE

An Epistolary Novel in Prose, Verse, and Image

Gabriela Anaya Valdepeña
& Richard Denner

Edited by Douglas James Martin

Scorpion Romance

dPress   Sebastopol
Darkness Visible Books   La Jolla
2008

First edition published in 2008 by:

Scorpion Romance
A subsidiary of dPress
www.dpress.net

in collaboration with:

Darkness Visible Books
P.O. Box 577
La Jolla, CA 92038
darknessvisiblebooks@yahoo.com

All photographs included in letters from Gabriela Anaya del Alma and Jacques Bâtard were taken by Gabriela Anaya Valdepeña, except for the photo on page 18, taken by Caslyn Wells. All photographs included in letters from Rychard Artaud, Bouvard Pécuchet, and Jampa Dorje were taken by, or used by permission of, Richard Denner.

Many of the poems, prose excerpts, and images used here have been included in previous publications by dPress and Darkness Visible Books.

The Poetry House, pictured on page 96, is a construction in redwood and copper, by sculptor Bruce Johnson, and installed at Paradise Ridge Sculpture Garden, Santa Rosa, California.

The authors wish to thank Douglas James Martin for the poems written in the voice of Jacques Bâtard, John Bennett for an excerpt from his correspondence, and Harvey Goldner for his cameo appearance, as well as for his immortal inflections.

FIRST EDITION

Printed in the United States of America

Library of Congress Control Number: 2008943304

ISBN: 978-0-9774000-2-7

In memory of Harvey Goldner, 1942–2007
and David Bromige, 1933–2009

Contents

The Correspondents

Gabriela Anaya del Alma. . . . . . . Damsel, Dancer, Dreamer.

Rychard Artaud . . . . Insurance Executive, Publisher, Opium Eater.

Bouvard Pécuchet . . . . Seeker, Runaway, Tree Planter.

Jampa Dorje (né Jubal Dolan) . . Hunter, Bookstore Proprietor, Monk.

Jacques Bâtard. . . . . Scholar, Adventurer.

Harvey Goldner . . . . Cab Driver, Seattle Sage.

PROLOGUE

From: Jacques Bâtard
To: Rychard Artaud
Sent: Wednesday, May 24, 2006 8:12 PM
Subject: your better nature

I do not trust you, and I never have,
though circumstances must, at times, forgive
where friends would not. And we were friends, of sorts,
if borrowed bail discharged to sundry courts
could purchase friendship. But all that was then,
though now I must, reluctantly, again,
bet on your better nature. There is a woman
at stake. You smile, I'm sure, to see my human
weakness crest at such a trivial cause;
but Alma is nothing like the giddy sows
we'd fuck with in the bars of Malibu.
No, she is beauty, fire, and sweetness, too,
compact with wit and deep imagination—
but enough of that, already—In summation:
she wishes to attend that conference
for poetry at Mills College where once
Bouvard and I contested to undo
the greatest share of eager ingenue
with glib iambics, metered masquerades,
bohemian masks, and lyrical charades.
And though my mighty Alma is more apt,
herself, to slay legions of fools rapt
in her own words, before she also die,

her frutifulness of fancy might supply,
to subtle hands, a highway to her heart.
What can I do then? Any time apart,
however brief, corrodes me like a fire,
but neither can I come, nor can deny her.
So that leaves you, as the unlikely guard
'gainst all usurpers, not the least Bouvard,
who may well be there too. And, if you please,
do not let slip, to Alma, that a disease
of fellowship once infected he and I;
that is, although a fact I can't deny,
a diagnosis she need never know.
I hold you, then, responsible, Artaud,
for keeping Alma safe from all design,
and do not forget that, though, like the divine,
I cannot, or will not, orchestrate it all,
and Alma must, like Eve, be free to fall;
I have reserved, as jealous Yahweh hath,
innumerable objects for my wrath.

I

JULY'S OFFERINGS

JULY 30TH–AUGUST 27TH

From: Rychard Artaud
To: Gabriela Anaya del Alma
Sent: Sunday, July 30, 2006 1: 22 PM
Subject: july's offerings

you can find the offering below on

http://www.melancholiastremulousdreadlocks.com

ALL I WANTED

All I wanted was to throw myself into the arms of a beautiful woman.
It was the night I went to hear Pony Poindexter.
She was coming up Grant Avenue with a sailor on her arm.
She hailed me but seemed embarrassed.
She recognized me from high school.
Same graduating class.
I drove the three of us to her place in the Height.
She took off for her bedroom with the sailor.
I sat on the wall-to-wall carpet, drank vodka and wrote poems.
Perfumed dreams.
She came out her room to tell me she didn't fuck the sailor.
He fell asleep in a chair getting undressed.
She loves me.
She's loved me for years.
We've been classmates since the third grade.
I can't place her.
She says she had always thought I was a sharp dresser.

She liked that my socks coordinated with my shirts.
I made that little fold on the waist of my Levis.
The *pachuco* look.
She loved me, but I couldn't fuck her yet.
But I could lick her pussy.
And would I help her get back to her sister's in Oakland.
Her pimp would be along soon.
I went and got a tire iron from my car for protection.
Her flesh excited me.
I wanted her blood in my veins.
Helped her pack.
Got all the stuff in my car.
Left the sailor on a stained sheet in the false dawn.

From: Gabriela Anaya del Alma
To: Rychard Artaud
Sent:v   Monday, July 31, 2006 11:34 PM
Subject: Re: july's offerings

Your poem had nuances of *Taxi Driver*. It was seamless.

I love your voice, you know.

Gabriela

From: Rychard Artaud
To: Gabriela Anaya del Alma
Sent: Tuesday, August 01, 2006 1: 22 PM
Subject: in bad taste

was the poem altogether unsavory, or was it just the right amount of sleaze?

From: Gabriela Anaya del Alma
To: Rychard Artaud
Sent: Tuesday, August 01, 2006 3:34 PM
Subject: Re: in bad taste

I didn't find it unsavory or sleazy, at all. I thought you were a very human prince in it, not the kind of emasculated prince I heard about in fairy tales growing up, having neither cock, nor balls, nor flaws, nor blood pressure.

From: Rychard Artaud
To: Gabriela Anaya del Alma
Sent: Friday, August 04, 2006 6:01 PM
Subject: pink mood poem

psychedelic pink psychodelphi
pink psychoracle lick pink ink pink
the color of lips the color
of the cheek the color of
intestines eyes of insects
wingéd bleeding things
in inner space
substantives hold their own
adjectives depend on substantives
holding their own

Ying/yang
yab/yum
tune-in/turn-on
a posteriori experience related
a fortiori in terms of significant
a priori synthesis
daisycrazy
turkeyjerkey

automatic replication analogue of
passion-beauty-love

analytic intersubjective meta-aleatoric patramorphesis

on the blue pole of the South Moon
Venus has a hot cushion

P.S. bouvard asked me to send you his greetings, and his apologies

From: Gabriela Anaya del Alma
To: Rychard Artaud
Sent: Friday, August 04, 2006 6:31 PM
Subject: Re: pink mood poem

Ha! I had no idea I would inspire you. I'm thrilled! And I'll put this poem next to the photo. I love how it blends all together, becoming soft and out of focus, like an old photograph, like friendship. The words you chose make rich sounds; they are fun for my mouth to read out loud.

I am taking the liberty of sending you a poem for Bouvard, the one for the radio photo he liked so much. I know he detests computers. Please see that he gets this.

The Air is Alive

The air is alive with news of you today.
I know, I was to meet you at the old
Venus café, behind the Shriner's Lodge,
in the shabby center of Sebastopol.
But there have been birthdays, and eighteen long stem roses
died in my arms, and my lost shepherd herded
twelve and a half soccer players and their ball.

12

No wool was shorn, and not a goal was scored,
and I'm running out of excuses once again.

We're on and off, like The Clapper, like a bra.
My heart is heavy as your letter press,
and my fingers are stained. I want to love you
deaf, or blind, and anything but sane,
while trees and dollars wither in the drought,
while unpicked almonds roast in their narrow shells.
And I would have visited you in the asylum, but I
was not yet a thought, much less an arm, much less
this woman disarmed by your unending song.

Did Bouvard ever get my poem? Give this image to him too. Tell him I miss him. Tell him I might accept his apologies. Tell him I might never understand him.

Gabriela

From: Rychard Artaud
To: Gabriela Anaya del Alma
Sent: Monday, August 14, 2006 8:08 PM
Subject: ran into bouvard

I saw Bouvard in the Venus Café. He looked beat, had an unhealthy pallor. I ordered a latté and started toward the garden outside, but Bouvard waved and I joined him, sat and waited for him to unburden himself. Women chatting on our right were dressed in black, a contingent of the Women in Black, back from their silent vigil. Words from my mouth, for instance, these women in black, already altered, because my description only hints at their experience.

"It's my muse," Bouvard said, "she's a liar with a camera, and her photos have come alive and speak to me. She is full of painterly poses, full of the effects of light and dark, and because of this, there's a tension created about her posing, about the posing of the photographer in her own pictures. She poses herself naked and without agenda, so no matter how she situates herself, she is the artist both within the frame and without. Hers is a fresh sophistication arising from natural innocence."

He opened a portfolio, and I looked at a few of her photos. The well-defined poses became their essence and merged with my words. The presence of her image was palatable. Racism, war, suffering, love, humor, the planets in their revolutions, everything was subsumed. A shadow, an element of excess, fell across Bouvard's brow. He touched one photograph with his index finger and sneered, "This is post-modern modernity, a piece of cardboard standing in for a woman."

Bouvard was definitely in torment. He continued, "I feel like I'm in a hell realm, surrounded by rotten corpses, and there are walls of fire in every direction. I'm splayed on the molten ground, where my body is cut by searing saws. Then, the pieces reassemble, and I am cut apart again."

Surely he exaggerated. But he replied, "No, this is not the half of it. I quote Petrarch: 'My life is steeped in cureless grief,' but the thorn that gouged Francesco was a mere sliver to the timber that tortures me." From a speaker in the corner of the room I heard the statue music from Mozart's Don Juan. I decided to let my friend wallow in his despair. Anything I said would be peripheral. Besides, Bouvard seemed perversely to enjoy his agony, so I apologized for having to run, finished off my latté, and headed for the gym.

From:	Gabriela Anaya del Alma
To:	Rychard Artaud
Sent:	Tuesday, August 15, 2006 10:19 AM
Subject:	Re: ran into bouvard

Rychard,

Tell Bouvard I have sought out Pancho Villa to comfort me. Since he lost his cojones he has been very tender; he nestles in the curve of my hip and sleeps. I've no idea what he dreams of, or if he dreams, at all. His teeth are narrow, like the edges of time. He chases Baudelaire around the room until he is listless, an amorphous defeated planet.

I turned 43 yesterday, and celebrated with The Cure's *Love Song,* though Baudelaire whined through the first half. The last part was clear though—the bass punched like Bouvard's heart.

From: Rychard Artaud
To: Gabriela Anaya del Alma
Sent: Tuesday, August 15, 2006 12:42 PM
Subject: Re: she has sought out pancho villa

she has sought out pancho villa to comfort her, he sleeps in the curve of her hip, they have taken his cojones, but so what? she strokes his fur and wonders of what he dreams, why dream? he is in the best of dreams, could dream no further, except to lick her ankles

From: Gabriela Anaya del Alma
To: Rychard Artaud
Sent: Wednesday, August 16, 2006 6:55 AM
Subject: Cojones in the Heart

Pancho's cojones are in his heart. His largesse, his loyalty fortify me. And yet, I know, you could distract him with a fine filet, long enough for your friend, whose pain amuses you, to steal my kisses. There is no official punishment for such a crime, I am thinking. Baudelaire looks up at me from his rawhide with a prayer in his eyes: "May God grant you the grace to fashion a few beautiful verses which will prove to you that you are not the lowest of maidens, that you are not inferior to those you despise."

Are you happy now? You've got me writing before the sun.

 Grrrrrrrrrrr!

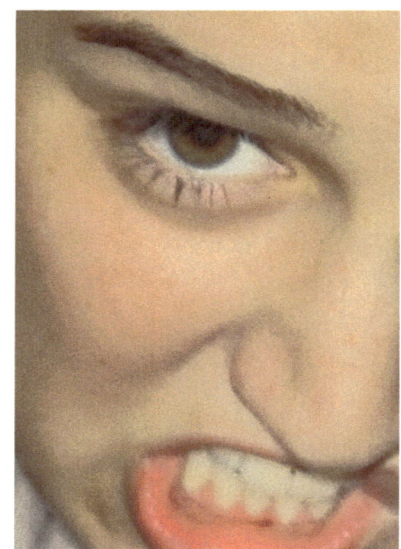

From: Gabriela Anaya del Alma
To: Rychard Artaud
Sent: Thursday, August 17, 2006 11:08 AM
Subject: Minsky's

Hi Rychard,

I am so lucky. I found this white bowler hat yesterday at the thrift store! I got the balloon for my birthday, along with a dozen red roses. As you can see, I'm in my birthday suit.

From: Gabriela Anaya del Alma
To: Rychard Artaud
Sent: Saturday, August 19, 2006 4:39 PM
Subject: Mexican Blondes

Here is another one you can show to Bouvard:

From: Rychard Artaud
To: Gabriela Anaya del Alma
Sent: Tuesday, August 22, 2006 11:43 AM
Subject: Re: Mexican Blondes

dear gabriela,

bouvard sends you this message:

> We've both been up all night long.
> I have a lot to tell you, but I'm afraid to begin.
> I've flipped my wig, but your blondness gives me courage.
> My words are both true and false,
> and I live in between, yearning.

From: Gabriela Anaya del Alma
To: Rychard Artaud
Sent: Thursday, August 24, 2006 9:11 AM
Subject: Re: Mexican Blondes

You can tell Bouvard that my blondness is temporary, like the gift of my heart. But these words will always be his:

> The prom queen had a penis. I didn't know.
> I would have been that much more
> jealous.
> Penis envy? No.
> Men lack the feminine quality she had,
> something that makes dirty angels, like me,

breathe,
something that dainty devils, like me,
need
to spread ourselves
open.
The boys had their chance with me when I was homely.
They're sorry now that I'm blonde. Store-bought
bouquets sink in tall vases. I'm feverish
yet they feed me with cold. Of course,
I never stabilize.

From: Bouvard Pécuchet
To: Gabriela Anaya del Alma
Sent: Saturday, August 26, 2006 10:38 AM
Subject: Re: Hardly stable

Dear Anya,

I've been taking a much needed break from email the past few days and will continue to do so until Monday or Tuesday of next week, or maybe the next millennium, while I work on my manuscript. (Then I'll have a thousand or a trillion to open!) But I saw the photo of you with that blonde wig and holding a rose on my desktop today, and I just have to thank you one more time (at least) for the beauty you bring to my life. I appreciate you so much.

I visited the old Venus Cafe. Rychard was there. He sat patiently and listened to my lament. He is a kind soul, but I know he finds me tiresome. I imagine you in a white room with white shoes. I dare look no further; my eyes burn. The light here dazzles. I bet Pancho Villa sits in your lap! The hero of the revolution. O, Villa. V for Vendetta. We are two Vs behind their masks. Voltage. Strong medicine. Well, it's the movies.

My research continues. The Colmecs living near the redwoods in the area around the Bohemian Grove planted trees in the shape of a mandala and dedicated the space to the Source of Light. Like Stonehenge. A Calendar of Trees. A sacred grove. Planted Redwoods like the Druids planted Oak. My grandfather, Bouvard Luis Fécuchet, was to be murdered in the Bohemian Grove by a band of Masons. He was on the verge of having his stomach slit open and his intestines pulled out and his body fed to the beasts of the field for revealing his secret, when an arrow pierced his heart. Going to have his guts spilled for spilling his guts, and at a timely moment—a mercy killing. But I can't go into this now.

Your lips' red. Your forearms—white in white gloves. The light is like white sand in a clear river. My pride, that is, my lust, sees you clearly.

My grandfather, the great archeoastronomer, used twin compasses to determine the precession of the equinox in the Sacred Grove of the Thirty-three. We are twin compasses circling one another in eternity, and five minutes ago, and now. We are on a pilgrimage to the Martyr's shrine.

I'm delighted. Hardly stable…tormented. Like in a great storm, ravished...

In rapture,

Bouvard

From:	Gabriela Anaya del Alma
To:	Rychard Artaud
Sent:	Sunday, August 27, 2006 9:07 AM
Subject:	urgent! (for Bouvard)

Yesterday Bouvard emailed me directly. I was not expecting that.

I have fought with Jacques, and I have been out all night. If you see Bouvard, please give him this letter:

Dear Bouvard,

I've left him, finally. He bought the wrong shade of nail polish—
he got classic red; I asked for chaotic.

He's obsessed with Caesar, and insects. He spies on them, then
paints them on a two inch square canvas. I wrote him this poem;
it didn't make any difference:

I Said

We were bored. I said:
we can photograph ants, if you want to,
carrying their bones on their backs
as they crawl on the red asphalt
in search of crumbs.

Some days
your crumbs have been
my only feast.
How quickly
the heart expands, needs still more
to fill it. I said:

we can photograph ants. We can
walk with our bare feet over

hot stones. We can sit
on the curb, like honey,
all day.

The oils drove him mad—must have been the oils; we ran out of vodka last
week. I bribed a blue jay to shit on his brush, and after that vengeance is
God's.

Yes! I'll meet you, somewhere, for one beer. Will you come?

II

TO THE CLOISTER

AUGUST 28TH–SEPTEMBER 10TH

From: Bouvard Pécuchet
To: Gabriela Anaya del Alma
Sent: Monday, August 28, 2006 12:50 PM
Subject: Re: last photo

I imagined you in white, but I see now it was a shade of yellow you're wearing. Well, I got the shoes right, and Pancho Villa is in his place near your hip. Imagine, leaving you alone like that with an unfinished beer. Where was he off to? You wait, and the roses wilt. What wilt thou do?

Ask for chaotic, and you get it. I'll paint ants with you, right after I finish my rendition of this Amphisbaena. At the edge of desire, a two-headed snake seduces me, and I can feel its arms, tiny bony blokes. Sure, I know that creature from the lagoon, that's yr mother, and after the nuclear bombs and poison gas steroids and aids, the survivors are the meek, them at the bottom of the heap, who adopt a new Eden, moma and dada, and live there, in the junk heap.

Some claim the Amphisbaena has a head at both ends, but others argue this would be impossible because there would be no former part of its body. I'm of the opinion my snake has two heads the better to cover you with kisses.

Besame,

Bouvard

From: Gabriela Anaya del Alma
To: Rychard Artaud
Sent: Wednesday, August 30, 2006 10:44 AM
Subject: for Bouvard, again

Rychard,

I'm sorry to keep involving you like this. Bouvard sent me another email, but I still find it hard to communicate with him directly.

Tell him that if he doesn't decide to show, soon, I might stand him up when he does. And he may never get another chance.

Tell him I would make a warm wife, though my hair may strangle him in the night. Tell him his grandfather was lucky; not everyone gets a *coup de grace*.

30

From:	Rychard Artaud
To:	Gabriela Anaya del Alma
Sent:	Wednesday, August 30, 2006 1:12 PM
Subject:	Re: bouvard cloistered

dear anya,

bouvard has left sebastopol to carry on his researches in a tranquil retreat, so he tells me, i sent your message and the photo to him via jampa, one of his oldest friends, and mine, and now his spiritual adviser, the photo i put in a sealed envelope, as jampa is a monk, but he will deliver your missive more readily than i, since he knows where bouvard is cloistered

i know it is hard for you to understand bouvard's torment, indeed to fathom it would be to suffer, and as jampa loves to say, who needs suffering? jampa sent me this poem he wrote about bouvard and asked me to deliver it to you

BOUVARD CLOISTERED

He found tranquility
in a world warmed by an inner sun,
in a room beyond this very arch,
where he painted those amazing letters:

Jacob facing Esau in an initial F.
David lifting up his soul in an initial O.
The Treasures of the Church in an R.
Virgin and Child in a C.
Christ with his cross in an L.
The kiss of Judas in an A.
Resurrection in an initial U.

A dove in a D.
The skinning alive of St. Bartholomew on an initial I.
The Elevation of the Host in an initial A.

In spite of the many poems he dedicated to women,
it is not to be assumed Bouvard was a womanizer;
in fact, it is not known whether or not he had sex.

From references in his poems,
he had sex twice, which is not much.
I've had sex ten times, and let me tell you,
I can see what people like about it.

Now, over here, on this bench,
he extracted gallotannic acid from oak galls,
which he then mixed with ferrous sulfate,
gum, water, and color to prepare his inks.

32

the poem ends abruptly

i have no idea how bouvard will respond to the odalisque, but i feel it is best not to censure things and hide them from him

wishing you all the best,

rychard

From: Rychard Artaud
To: Gabriela Anaya del Alma
Sent: Wednesday, August 30, 2006 1:26 PM
Subject: Re: bouvard cloistered

dear anya,

jampa is embarrassed to tell you that he just sent an earlier "claudia" version of his poem, he wished he knew if there was a correct protocol for dedicating the same poem to different women, but of course his ignorance is to be expected of monks in the order of the novanaieve

here is the corrected section:

      Jacob facing Esau in an initial F.
      David lifting up his soul in an initial O.
      The Treasures of the Church in an R.
      Virgin and Child in a G.

Christ with his cross in an A.

The kiss of Judas in a B.

Resurrection in an initial R.

A dove perching on an I.

The flagellation of a penitent against an E.

The skinning alive of St. Bartholomew on an initial L.

The Elevation of the Host in an initial A.

From: Gabriela Anaya del Alma
To: Rychard Artaud
Sent: Wednesday, August 30, 2006 3:50 PM
Subject: Trinity

Rychard,

Only Bouvard has ever called me *Anya*. I'm uncomfortable that you know that name.

And don't believe he has only had sex twice. He loves to fool monks, and women, and poets. Bouvard knows, if I had let him, that night he anointed me Anya beneath the drifting Oakland moon, that I would have been the last, but certainly not the third.

I have never heard of Claudia, but I do know that all the women Boo has known are mere elaborations of me. I am a woman for all the positions of the sun, a *Belle de Jour* for every hour. I have more shades than fire. I'm tender and strong at the same time; none of that either/or Kierkegaard crap.

Thank you for concealing my photo from Jampa, that dear and holy man. Bouvard is the only man whose morals I need to smash. He gave me his mutant cross that night, and asked for it back the next morning. I wrote him this poem, but it didn't make any difference:

You Can't Take It Back

In your living room
a mooch sleeps,
snores in time
to the cacophony of spirits.
Don't say it.
Don't say it;
you want back what you gave.
I can resurrect
dead heroes;
I can make hunks
from romance novels
kiss my feet.
This is a superficial world;
not even the seas are deep enough.
You, with your assemblage
of *borrachos*,
mooches, and *mujeres*.
I did not; I did not
make you swear it:

amor,
love—
four letter words—
you closed your eyes,
kissed your mutant cross.
and put it around my neck.

The History of the Mutant Cross:

Bouvard told me that his mother was a Catholic and his father was a Protestant, who converted to please his mother. But then his mother met a Baptist preacher, and he saved her so that she stayed saved. His father refused to convert again. The Catholic church was too much fun. He drank a lot and beat Bouvard. His mother made him burn his Beatles and Elvis albums at a rock n roll record burning party, at the church.

When Bouvard turned twenty-six, he had the cross made in New Mexico, out of melted gold wedding bands he said he found one day on his steps—all different sizes, all different grades of gold. He had read all the engravings on the back of the bands and created a mantra out of them that he would recite every time he felt the inclination to be reborn or repent.

Why the two bars on the cross? Bouvard said each one cancels out the other religion.

I hope Jampa will not try to convert Bouvard. He would not make a good Buddhist. He is not holy. He is not an iconoclast either. He is not a tortured existentialist. He is what he is: afraid of the trinity of Gabriela, Anya, and Alma: mother, daughter, and spirit.

I am scared too.

Please, do not call me *Anya*, ever again.

Regards,

Gabriela Anaya del Alma

From: Rychard Artaud
To: Gabriela Anaya del Alma
Sent: Wednesday, August 30, 2006 5:12 PM
Subject: Re: bouvard not holy

dear gabriela,

please accept this sincere apology for my slip of the tongue, bouvard was constantly repeating that name, holy it is, like the tetagrammatron, the first syllable is the voice of praise, the final syllable is a halleluiah, the in and out breathing of spirit, yes, we must keep jampa in the dark, he is a willing servant, and i am sure he will not attempt to convert bouvard, as he is not an evangelical, merely a humble practitioner of the dharma, helping us all to find freedom

bouvard knows he is not holy, knows he is a slacker, but he needs a place of refuge, his decision to paint the letters of the alphabet is a welcome relief from

his hobby of painting hotrods, he is a master of the pinstripe and the sudden
flameout, also, the racetrack is not the place for him at present, so he's doffed
his double vest and donned a hair shirt

as for the poem embedded (choice word) with claudia, this was to whom
the poem by jampa was previously addressed, and he wants to clear up
any confusion, he would have changed the letters in the poem according to
bouvard's current devotion, but the ritual of monks is exhausting, and jampa
was careless this time and mixed up who he was envisioning

know this, though, jampa has only addressed the poem to two women, so the
integrity of the poem is not truly compromised, nor is bouvard's devotion to his
belle de jour, and this it is his sickness unto death

you relate the history of the mutant cross, the only cross bouvard is connected
to now is the tao cross of the hanged man in the upper arcana of the tarot, a man
at cross purposes

bouvard told you his mother was a convert to a fundamentalist faith, but did he
tell you she was a disciple of marie claire prophet, and that the exorcism they
committed on bouvard went well beyond the burning of his elvis and beatle
records? he had to attend the burning of a wicker man and incant the names of
the legions of rocknroll demons from buddy holly to mick jagger

the mantra bouvard constructed from the wedding bands he melted to make his
mutant cross happened to be the lost word of masonic lore, and so the curse of
his grandfather is attached to our bouvard

i am hoping your next intercourse will be with bouvard

yours,

rychard

Dearest Anya,

I am sorry Jampa sent you the poem about me with the Claudia inscription. He knows I detest cryptograms—a medieval conceit of his; he is always trying his hardest to obscure the most trivial details while in broad strokes revealing the best kept secrets. May this mani sayer have to roll snake eyes a million times in a row to get out the cold hell he will reside in for revealing my lost love, and now my torment of love.

I've continued my researches into the arcane mysteries surrounding my grandfather's demise, and spelled myself by painting four miniatures: Noah building the ark on the skeleton of a letter A (how they get the letter turned over is a mystery); next, plagues of locust and darkness swallowing the letter N (a dirge to my recent discovery that Anais Nin was a bigamist); then, the burning bush speaking to Moses in a Y (a Gnostic joke in this); and lastly, another A with Moses driving out the frogs for pharaoh (the pin stripe of royal blue along the edge of pharaoh's robe pleases me greatly).

The issue of the mutant cross surfaces, troubles me, returns me to those days, so few, so recent, so distant, and to my joy even when arguing with you, to your fire, your bright laughter, to the clarity of your words. I tremble, realizing how close I came to banishment; when you make a decision in the heat of passion you will always, I know, keep to your promise.

That cross was a talisman, like an antique spearhead which dreamed of killing a saber-tooth tiger, a cross which had been waiting for your neck, both compliant and powerful, and pleased to have fallen into your destiny. I only wanted it back to protect you from the consequences.

The pleasures of paradise are hidden from ascetics, because they would not understand them; but I am warming to your communiques, oblique though they be. Perhaps the fountains of Aganippe and Hippocrene run with fresh vigor.

yours all ways,

Boo

From:	Gabriela Anaya del Alma
To:	Bouvard Pécuchet
Sent:	Thursday, August 31, 2006 10:09 AM
Subject:	Corner of Your Mind

Dear Boo,

I have had to get work at the club again, since leaving Jacques. I need you. Will you ever see through your own indirections?

Corner Of Your Mind

I hope you were not expecting a monody.
You are not yet dead to me; your indecision
haunts the thin dream I had last night

You'll never rise to an apotheosis,
though you have become the water in my eyes.

I curse your curses, which keep us apart, Bouvard
of my heart, *de mi alma, de mis venas, mis uñas,*

41

mi sangre, mi ser. Misery is God's;
let him take it.

Come to me, my showy secret!
Give me back that cross, and yank your wrists
down from the nails in Claude's stretcher bars.

I still have two tickets to the game.
Apollo and Dionysus, so they say,
will likely go into overtime.
With our breath we will write our names
on the window at the back of the bus.

From: Jampa Dorje
To: Gabriela Anaya del Alma
Sent: Thursday, August 31, 2006 6:42 PM
Subject: prism of his mind

Jampa here, I'm not such a naif, I know what's going on, and I like my role
as Mercury. Today, I was in Bouvard's cell, and as I had my camera with
me, I shot a picture of one of his artworks, perhaps the brush in the right
corner of this assemblage is the bush he refers to as having repose in the
letter "y."

Rest easy Miss Gabriela, your presence is reflected in the prism of his mind.

Jampa

43

In Bouvard's art, I see all the things he is:
a coat of arms,
a chess game,
a short ladder that leads   They say desire is the root of all suffering,
to a phony alarm.   but this warmth,
                                                  which will not beg,
                                                  never subsides.

44

From: Rychard Artaud
To: Gabriela Anaya del Alma
Sent: Friday, September 01, 2006 4:01 PM
Subject: Re: Toby's Jubal

hi, gabriela,

i have just visited bouvard in the cloister, where I saw jampa arranging roses on his altar to the divine feminine, he had such a smile on his face, his is a happy soul, being bouvard's spiritual guide must please him

by the way, did you know that bouvard has written a harlequin romance? i have an extra copy, it is set in berkeley in the early 60s and was published last year by scorpion press, its title is -toby's jubal- and the blurb on the back reads

> *Toby had never been impetuous—until she escaped to Berkeley to marry a man whose words won her heart, but whose true nature she'd never seen.*

i'm attaching a picture of the cover—

Toby's Jubal
Bouvard Pécuchet
90 pages, perfect bound

Scorpion Romance 2006
A subsidiary of dPress

$12

From: Gabriela Anaya del Alma
To: Rychard Artaud
Sent: Saturday, September 02, 2006 12:31 PM
Subject: Re: send a copy

Please, send me a copy of his romance, if you have an extra. I can't get enough of him. I eat, drink, and sleep Bouvard.

xo,

Gabriela

From: Rychard Artaud
To: Gabriela Anaya del Alma
Sent: Saturday, September 02, 2006 4:45 PM
Subject: sending bouvard's book today

ok, gabriela, it's on it's way, today, might reach you midweek,

bouvard asked me to tell you, "I hope it will reach further, to the secret of your flower," not sure what he's alluding to, i'm only the mailman

xo,

rychard

From: Gabriela Anaya del Alma
To: Bouvard Pécuchet
Sent: Tuesday, September 05, 2006 3:16 PM
Subject: Re: Toby's Jubal

Dear Bouvard,

Jacques came 'round the club last night, pleading. Exes hanging around: bad for business. He cursed you as the bouncers threw him out. The following is written

Upon A Slow Rise

Meteors cannot be reasoned with.

You do not know the pressure
my knees have been under.

Stars do not have points
and they do not like
being drawn as such.

Just kidding,
they do not have thoughts,

only fits of fire.

I have many thoughts
unwinding like a galaxy,
as I rise in the aftermath
of a million backbends.

In the club, men love
to see a woman's ribs
accentuated, the fragile
arch of the neck as the
hair fans the floor.

Men cannot be reasoned with.

From: Gabriela Anaya del Alma
To: Bouvard Pécuchet
Sent: Friday, September 08, 2006 10:40 PM
Subject: **You're Brilliant!**

And so much fun! I was thrilled to receive the book today! I've been reading it on my breaks between sets. I've just come to a "HEAD BENDING DEAD END."

I adore you,

Anya

From: Bouvard Pécuchet
To: Gabriela Anaya del Alma
Sent: Saturday, September 09, 2006 12:27 PM
Subject: jubal's crash

"My memory is coming back," Jubal said,
"I must've hit my head on the steering wheel."
The officer replied, "from the looks of your rig you were flying,
probably doing eighty when you hit the crest of that hill
and it's lucky we weren't both killed."

Jubal looked at the wreckage, and it made him think
of all the money he had spent getting his car fixed up, after
the last wreck, which wasn't his fault—a friend had borrowed
his wheels to run an errand and had run instead right into a house.
But this WAS Jubal's fault, he had panicked and run from the law.

"Running a little late, damn it," he thought,
and him on probation after the fiasco with his friend,
and now he'd run six stop signs and driven off a cliff.
He was in for it, he guessed, was definitely fucked, yet
the officer seemed chipper enough, even though his car
had suffered major damage. Euphoria, Jubal supposed.

The flight to the bottom of the hill had been a trip, the sense
of free fall when the steering vanished. He remembered
the sensation of turning to the right and back to the left,
and the panicky feeling he had of being out of control,
and at the same time the need to make a split-second decision
as to whether to go between the pillars with the chain attached,
or to avoid them by turning left, as though it would be possible
to make a sharp left turn while traveling 80 mph through the air.

Left, he decided, and he turned hard, and it came to naught;
or it came to naught while he was aloft, but having the wheel
turned must've made the car go sideways when it hit
the cement pillars and flipped over and landed on its roof.

What Jubal couldn't remember was how he got from the car
to sitting on his ass in the middle of the street.
"You were damn lucky, you silly son of a bitch," said the cop,
"when that car flipped over those posts, you fell out
and the car rolled on. Shit, you might've drowned."

Jubal looked at the headlights, one pointing up and one down,
and another memory returned, the officer pointing a gun at him,

saying, "you stay right there, don't move," while he pulled himself
out the window of his cruiser. And Jubal remembered the wrenching
sound the axle had made when it stopped the vehicle,
and he remembered the strange, harmonic sound
the wire fence made, stretching to breakpoint.

None of this was music to his ears, but he was amazed
at the amount of information flooding back into his brain,
completely unrelated bits, clovis points that
appeared for a moment to wake his logically bemused self
to the design in the absurd drama of being alive.

When the gods are done with you, they melt you down for soap,
or they roll you up in a rug and smoke you. "Depends on what
you're made of," the officer said, "it was a dumb thing,
but you're alive; it could have been a head-bending dead end."

From: Gabriela Anaya del Alma
To: Bouvard Pécuchet
Sent: Sunday, September 10, 2006 2:37 PM
Subject: Crashes

Crashes are something you know a lot about Bouvard; keep writing about them.
The headlights—one pointing up, one pointing down—reminded me of a bad
boob job here. Capsular contraction—well there is more than one case of it. The
body rejects the foreign object, builds a bubble of scar tissue. My breasts, though,
are beckoning and soft.

So many crashes in my life, so many dead ends. So many starts, so few finishes.

> Everyone finds your breasts beckoning and soft.
> I look deeper, to your diamond heart's core.
> Dig it, your arched back and hair are my ruin and my salvation.
> Can't you see I'm one with the sea and a steady candle flame?
> I want to thank you for this beautiful and mysterious world.
> The notes climb from my mouth likes bubbles of bliss and grief,
> and many Gardens blow.

III

A WASTE OF SUN

SEPTEMBER 11TH–SEPTEMBER 22ND

From: Gabriela Anaya del Alma
To: Bouvard Pécuchet
Sent: Monday, September 11, 2006 2:37 PM
Subject: a waste of sun

What a waste of sun this day has been! Been cooped up in this noisy, windowless place since 11:00 a.m. I have decided day shift is less crazy. Tips aren't as good, but fewer drunks to deal with. I once dreamt of getting tipsy with you. But you are too holy now, at least in your own mind. Mondays are always bitter. Pour some sugar on me.

Monday

This is the day everything I have ever put off
comes home to crow. Two-faced pizza moonday,
you boast a borrowed light, and yet incite the sun
to mundane disputes over the week's management,
while werewolves howl in toadying mockery.
But Monday can malinger permanently, for all I care;
I'll glide gracefully into Tuesday without you!
Though you side with the rain, and plot against Zeus,
you are no match for me, after five cups of coffee.
Let the tide rule itself; I'll knock you off
that cratered perch with David's sling and a moonstone.
I'll shake you off like a clingy lover, Muckday, while you crawl
into Uranus to suck the sun's big, flaming cock!

57

Here is another story, not for Monday, or for Tuesday, but for Yesterday:

The Story of Impetuous Delirious Yesterday, by Bouvard Pécuchet

Impetuous Delirious Yesterday was born in Guayaquil, Ecuador, in the shadow of Mt. Higueroata, in 1970, a century and a half after the death of Simón Bolivar. Her mother, Juanita Bolivar Delirioso, is a descendent of that famous general. Her father, Jack Yesterday, who died of a drug overdose on the eve of the millennium, was an Englishman with a mysterious past, but with the means to guarantee that Impetuous would have every opportunity.

Impetuous attended school at the highly recommended San Martin Academy from the ages of eleven until seventeen. When she was sixteen, she became friends with a young man named Crisóstomo. No other name is known, and it is presumed this name is fictitious. It was through Crisóstomo that Impetuous met members of The Gurdjieff Society. Impetuous's parents learned of her friend through a correspondence with a concerned teacher. Fearing their daughter was associating with "known rebels" and in possible danger from the police, Impetuous was recalled from school. She swore the accusations were false and pleaded to return to the academy. Her parents were reluctant at first, but after a week, they relented.

A private detective was hired to watch her. The detective was to report her every move. She might well have been aware of the detective's presence, for shortly after her return to school, she went to the market with the detective following her. She was last seen in Guayaquil on April 1, 1997.

Floating between Hell and La Jolla, Impetuous became a street dancer. At first, her beauty and talent created incredulity, but it wasn't long before a rumor that she was dancing would create a furor of interest. She traveled extensively, and her dances made her into a legend, yet when agents and the media sought her, she was uninterested in their attentions and kept them at a distance. One cannot speak of her without echoing, however remotely, the monumental style of the Venezuelan dancer, Samantha. Impetuous is yet to have her name on a street sign, but she is yet to have people throw eggs at her, as well.

In the Summer of 2006, Impetuous met the famous Plagiarist poet, Rychard Artaud, at Mills College in Oakland, California. He was inspired to write the following poem, which I present here.

CONCUBINE OF THE NIGHT

Touched by her careless glance,
I write with blue lipstick.

Under a lot of pressure, she's trapped in the furniture.
She's a kissing girl who dances a mad dance.

She has a bad girl's sparkle in her innocent smile.
The doctor forgot to spank her when she was born.

She has sojourned to the moon and beyond.
Feverish, unstable, bruised, she wishes to be an echo.

Her wild thoughts hover, invisible as irony.
Losing her, I've discovered everything.

I can see myself in the thinly veiled Impetuous, but I'm still wondering who your Jubal is modeled after?

Hi, Miss Gabriela,

This is Jampa; I am monitoring Bouvard's computer while he is doing research. I have my own personal settings, but I know his passwords too and can navigate at will; thus I came across your email.

You may not know this, but Bouvard models his Jubal Dolan character on my youthful adventures. Your question inspired me to reminisce about the parallels between my early life and that of our friend's hero in his romantic novels. I've included a couple of photos that are Bouvard's favorites.

On the left, Jubal is following in the footsteps of Hemingway, posing as deer slayer, and on the right is the hunter with his pets. Here you see Jubal as killer and Jubal as friend to hind, in the footsteps of Sir Thomas Wyatt: *whoso list to hunt? I know where is an hind! but as for me, alas, I may no more.*

And below is one more photo, of "Jubal" today, reading with the estimable David Bromige, at Many Rivers.

From: Gabriela Anaya del Alma
To: Jampa Dorje
Sent: Wednesday, September 13, 2006 9:11 AM
Subject: Re: whoso list to hunt

Would "Jubal" be offended if I said he was handsome?

Gabriela

From: Jampa Dorje
To: Gabriela Anaya del Alma
Sent: Wednesday, September 13, 2006 9:51 AM
Subject: Re: whoso list to hunt

I think that your saying that I am handsome is flattering, and though a monastic I take it you mean it as a compliment: *hand some* but *hands off* is your intention. I do feel warmed by your thoughts.

Jampa

From: Gabriela Anaya del Alma
To: Jampa Dorje
Sent: Thursday, September 14, 2006 9:32 AM
Subject: Re: whoso list to hunt

Dear Jampa,

I am glad I do not offend you. Has my dear Bouvard begun now to cut his hair like you? If only I could have been his Delilah. Oh I am. But he is blind already and refutes his own strength.

I dreamed I visited you, Jampa, and you longed to kiss me, and cursed me for it. I retired to the guest chamber. You had a water bed. My sleep was very unstable, at first. But then you came to sit beside my closed door. Your mantra was a lullaby. I feel new this morning, free to dream of new sins.

Forgive me.

From: Jampa Dorje
To: Gabriela Anaya del Alma
Sent: Thursday, September 14, 2006 10:41 AM
Subject: visited in dreams

Oh, Miss Gabriela, 'twas not you I cursed in your dream, but myself. I knew you meant no harm; indeed, I knew you had come to assist my path. I am often visited in dreams by dakinis in many apparitional forms, sometimes wrathful, sometimes peaceful, and sometimes ecstatic; but no sky walker has ever been as attentive in helping to intensify and elevate my realization of the unity of pleasure and emptiness by the mix of your higher and lower energies.

I am a monk, but I cannot help but feel a certain bliss at the awareness that, for Bouvard, my earlier incarnations have the archetypal look of his romantic alter ego. Here are two more: Jubal circa 1960 with his 52 Chevy, and later in 1976.

From: Gabriela Anaya del Alma
To: Jampa Dorje
Sent: Friday, September 15, 2006 11:42 AM
Subject: Cupid, Hemingway, Miller; Love, Shadows, Madness

Bullets from that rifle are nothing compared to Cupid's blind arrows.

Cupid

He can't shoot straight,
though Cupid knows
we were meant to be.

Robin Hood's school
won't charge Cherubs,
and Cupid's too proud
for charity.

Stalemate.
Stale me.

Damn his pride.
Damn his bad aim.

Last time I saw Bouvard in a dream, he left suddenly, without kissing that spot
behind my knee. He left as if he had gotten news his prize steer had just gotten

loose, or his lucky horse had finally come in. Suddenly, he was disoriented by possibilities.

> Would Helen of Troy
> lament such an abrupt exit,
> or give it a second thought?
> Ernest Hemingway,
> off into the sunset—
> already,
> I've pondered it too much.
>
> NO!
> not Hemingway!
>
> Give me Henry Miller,
> a man who will love
> whoever is near him,
> and I will never leave his side.

Bouvard is the only man I know who panics when the news is good. He reacts equally to success or tragedy. He prefers the comfort of certain, uneventful, and constant low-grade misery. The thing he longs for most, he already has, if only he would decide to have it. Only one thing is certain: Death is blind, but cannot be cheated. In Love there is hope. Love is myopic, but wears glasses. Love is deaf, but reads sign language.

Shadows Sign

I hold my eyes in reverence
to the parlor of dutiful shadows
that honor you in sign language.
Each one holds its hands
frozen in a letter of your name.
Of this I am twice sure,
reading also their lips,
as I once read your kiss,
when shadows perished
in the equilibrium of our light.

From: Jampa Dorje
To: Gabriela Anaya del Alma
Sent: Saturday, September 16, 2006 8:23 PM
Subject: dreams, shadows, signs

You may be Bouvard's Delilah, but you are my vajrayogini, helping me retain a constant cognition of the primal purity of experience. Such desire is pure pleasure:

> The water bed you lay on in your dream was the lake of awareness.
> The offering of your body served as ransom for all sentient beings.
> Such a gift acts as a catalyst for a yogi's true practice to emerge.
> A knife in the water cuts through discursive thought.

From: Gabriela Anaya del Alma
To: Jampa Dorje
Sent: Sunday, September 17, 2006 3:51 PM
Subject: Re: desire is pure pleasure

Jampa,

Is desire ever pure? Does pure desire exist? I can't even remember the details of the last day I spent with Jacques, before I left him, but I can still taste the disappointment of having woken in my own bed this morning to the sound, not of your delicious mantras, but of a persistent mocking bird who has learned to sing like a car alarm.

I will not dance at the club tomorrow. Tomorrow I shall find three graces and photograph them in China silk veils while they sing death songs in the garden to honor Thanatos. Don't worry, we will live forever, you and I.

Bouvard who?	Oh Bouvard!
The pain of forgetting.	Forgetting what?

P.S. I have changed my dance name, once again, to Zephyr, the name of the west wind.

From: Rychard Artaud
To: Gabriela Anaya del Alma
Sent: Monday, September 18, 2006 12:24 PM
Subject: Re: shadow sign

> shadow sign
> secret sign
> a wave of grace
> see it in the poet's hollow
> see it in the firefly's glow
> see it in the roots and branches
> don't ask
> walk fast
> talk last

Jampa came to visit early this morning, clutching your recent correspondence, which he shared, he looked to me more like Jubal than monk, and yet all he could talk about was the past and present sufferings of Bouvard. I summarize:

> in the shadow of madness can be seen the face of god
> bouvard saw this face reflected in the knives his friend joe
> stuck in the tent pole and in the floor and in the table
>
> joe's dad was a friend of bouvard's grandfather
> and these two and hem and coop, that's gary cooper,
> used to hunt in idaho, not my idaho, but their idaho
>
> it was cupid's arrow that pierced the elder bouvard's heart
> a coup d'grace or a mercy killing, hard to know, but better

than having your heart torn out and fed to the birds of prey

this is not a miller's tale, nor is it the spew of a misogynist
bouvard searches for the mystery behind the mystery
and is perfecting the skill of retaining his seed

he realizes if his seed-essence is actually lost
his is the karma of killing a buddha
so, he is doing his best to maintain self-control

it was his prize steer that came in
and it was his favorite horse that was lost
he would like to kiss your knees, back and front

what he has is lost, everything but his good looks
death may not tolerate a cheat, but death likes a magician
ed dorn told me that the first tenant of magic is style

one's style of dying is what gives purpose to the future
know this, dakini queen of pure awareness
the supreme being is the dakini queen

in that shot of jubal in bermuda shorts
his rifle over his shoulder, next to the 52 chevy
that he totaled at the bottom of diamond pond

are those antlers in the basket of his bike?

i have been assisting Bouvard, occasionally, with his researches, especially
concerning the mysterious death of his grandfather, Bouvard Luis Pecuchet.

I recently found this photo of that eminent scholar of archeoastronomy in the archives of the Ellensburg Lodge of Free and Accepted Masons. He is walking in a parade, circa 1930, second from left, bearded and wearing the lambskin apron of a mason, the masons have many secret signs and shadowy secrets

From: Gabriela Anaya del Alma
To: Rychard Artaud
Sent: Tuesday, September 19, 2006 12:42 PM
Subject: Mass Confusion

My Dear Rychard,

I know I should not tempt Jampa. He doesn't understand my involuntary power. And Bouvard, what a fool he is! I am secular, I am holy. Though I appeal to his complexes, he will have to fight Heaven and Hell simultaneously to have this great piece of fiction.

I am to be read, in the open, where I hide. Wish him luck on my behalf. If you should need me, Rychard, I'm just a whisper away—

an ocean,

a galaxy,

a prayer,

a tantric touch.

xo,

Zephyr

From: Jampa Dorje
To: Gabriela Anaya del Alma
Sent: Wednesday, September 20, 2006 12:19 PM
Subject: Re: desire as pure pleasure

Dear Miss Gabriela,

If you have eradicated your negative proclivities, everything is pure, and desire becomes the wisdom of discernment. And yet, I can tell from your questions that you grasp at illusions; thus your suffering is intensified by the loss of a love in the past and the entertainment of a love in the future, and in your despair you worship at the altar of oblivion. But, I hasten to inform you, I have a message from Bouvard. Maybe it is a ruse, but he says your shape shifting and imprecations have touched him, and he will contact you personally, as soon as he comes in from his harvesting of huckleberries on the sky trail.

Here he comes now, his fingers dark with the juices of summer bounty. I compassionately leave you,

Jampa

From: Bouvard Pécuchet
To: Gabriela Anaya del Alma
Sent: Wednesday, September 20, 2006 1:04 PM
Subject: Troupe Rose

Ah, Zephyr is it now? I'd know you, Anya, in any tangle of scarves. You never cease to amaze and delight, and you have Jampa completely off balance with your juggling of sentiments.

Yes, though it has been a while since I contacted you directly, I have been reading your correspondences with Jampa. By taking advantage of his natural inquisitiveness and experience in espionage, I have allowed you, through Jampa, fairly comprehensive access to my work. Much that you have read in my romance, *Toby's Jubal*, is not fiction, but is instead a sequence of hagiographical occurrences of the old Jampa in a parallel universe. I now have in my possession a photo of a 1952 customized Chevrolet that is a duplicate of the one Jubal destroyed attempting to defy the laws of gravity.

Our kisses may have been postponed, but they will never crumble to the sea; they are meteors which perpetually orbit the heavenly lair of lovers, no years lost, no tears lost. Together we know what to do, know inspiration is a leak of awareness. Here, I am surrounded by dakinis, but I am not fazed by their charms nor in fear of their terrors. As Jampa Dorje has revealed to me, the Dakini is the vast and limitless expanse of emptiness, and on the ultimate level, the Dakini is beyond gender. All the same, it is a way space can manifest.

So, you can see how my work progresses. I attach a photo of *Troupe Rose*, the *Dancing Dakinis of the Four Winds*. I hope you have not forgotten that the celestial *Four Winds*, the troupe of troupes, is led by none other than the only Zephyr of my heart, but for now I must serve these apprentice dakinis, until their energy is under control and they have fulfilled their pledges of initiation. I will leave you here; the gong has rung in the gompa, and I must cross the charnel grounds to the far temple.

Bouvard! Where have you been? I regret so much that I cannot write more. I must run to find my three graces before they disappear with the sun.

I read your missives through a mist of tears. I wear black today for all the deaths unnoticed, for our resurrected love. When my search is done, I'll return to read your thoughts a hundred more times. Oh Bouvard. Even if I find those holy, happy women, I know tomorrow I will wake again, hungry, only to return to that

dreadful den of wine, dancing, and men who are not you. Bouvard, I love you as I have never wanted to love anyone.

Your Anaya, Your Zephyr, Your Voice.

For All The Deaths Unnoticed

Neither bury me in excess, nor embellish my tomb.
You know I want to live simple in Eden. Swallow me up,
or still the stars and grant them penance.

The sea is not deliberate, and yet you love her. I am
tortured by this rhetoric, and yet you torture me more.
I am certain of the sun, and yet you pinch my arm.

So I wear black for all the deaths unnoticed. Bequeath your
insolence to the moon, for she has waned into benevolence.
Time is a ghost that must resume its flight.

From: Bouvard Pécuchet
To: Gabriela Anaya del Alma
Sent: Wednesday, September 20, 2006 9:20 PM
Subject: to Anya from Bouvard

When I kiss you my heart is everywhere, existing in everything,
and there is misery, but more the torture of image than of person,
my head in your lap turning into a fish swimming in the deep, blue sea.

My eyes float at the level of your waist. So much to learn. Your legs,
your arms, and hands, your breasts, your lips are an idea of things,
fused with my desire to touch you and the secret music of an embrace.

Naked, I am a priest, and I consecrate the union of our desires,
while caresses preach of clouds and winds and virginal first fruits,
a gospel of trees and terraces and dazzling wings.

Up to now, I have been afraid of giving everything away,
of even looking in your direction, and I have acted the chimera,
with lion head, goat body and tail of snake, creature of imagination.

It's no wonder that after only one kiss, one slip of your tongue
in my mouth, I feel I will never escape, and that this slip of tongue
may betray us; the sun will rise and our dalliance be discovered.

Sister and mother and lover, child and wizened one combined,
we go together like beasts to water, although kisses never slake our thirst.
Darling, I am not sure I can endure this, and the whole world wonders.

From earth to sky, from alpha to omega, from the tips of my fingers
to your pink, misted contours, we find ourselves in constant longing,
and now it is September in Sebastopol, and you are in San Diego,

and I have grown drunk envisioning you, and I have lost control,
bewitched by your torrential song, writhing in these sensual flames.

Boo,

The fates have turned against me. The three graces don't want to know my name. I can't even send you their image; the attachment won't go through. Don't make waves in a surf town. You never warned me. A kiss is in order.

I'm in love with every man; I'm in love only with you. *On this side paradox; on the other, lobotomy.* The summer ants have overstayed their welcome, and are crawling on my comb. What I'd give if you would take my hair down and untangle it with your gentle fingers.

It's still warm enough for a bikini, but it's Thursday, and I am finished, though these poems must carry on.

Thursday

The week is yet inchoate; that is Thursday's charm.
Still time to disarm hearts, to slow the earth's rotation,
to introduce clouds to sky, to carve the Aztec calendar,
to form the very universe from mist. Humble Thursday
refused to let the week begin with his own name.
But let Jupiter swallow Kronos! This day alone
can promise sun, and on this day I could lose my dread
for all things cold. Ennui, carry me on your flaccid wings.
The euphoria of full flight is imminent and sure as death,
which must also be a kind of flying. Let my limbs trust
this breeze; my eyes will trust that light will never blind,
and every day is Thursday and I am never finished.

Dear Bouvard,

I will never be able to send the photo of The Graces. My little house of whispering candles has been ransacked and some of my files stolen. I have been warned by the base and vile husband of one of the three sisters that, should any photos of his wife surface, he will have me beheaded in the center of Tijuana's Revolución in broad daylight.

Rumor is she was once an Indian princess and savant. I had a dream yesterday that I would see her and her sisters, and alas it happened just that way. I happened upon them frolicking in her garden, a rare and glorious moment for a liar with a camera. She was soon escorted by her golden hair to a kept lair, plump with gold and red silk and antique Persian rugs, to be tortured endlessly with Wagner, wine, and all manner of delicious aphrodisiacs. But they could no more whet her appetite for her captor than saltpeter could a sailor's.

I have kept one hidden copy of this serendipitous, yet prophetic, capture. Someday, when we are alone, I will show it to you. As long as that photograph lives, she is free, in some other realm far from the rancid toad whose only hope for love is that she suddenly, after many decades, develops Stockholm Syndrome. I am on a hunger strike hoping to appease the gods. May they grant her freedom, in dreams and in life.

Incidentally, if you happen to buy me those silk tap pants I've craved, get them in a size one.

Love,

Anya

81

From: Bouvard Pécuchet
To: Gabriela Anaya del Alma
Sent: Friday, September 22, 2006 10:17 AM
Subject: Re: disturbing news

Dearest Anya,

I realize how distraught you are over the developments regarding your photos of the Three Graces, and I thought I would console you with Jampa's insight about the symbolic meaning of your recent experience. You will find his message appended below. I will leave you in his capable hands and return to work on the projects that he has assigned me. Milarepa is my guide.

I love you,

Bouvard

Here is Jampa's text. It begins with a prayer.

> Hum.
> Right in Northwest Ogyan, there,
> on a lotus pistil stem,
> powers amazing and supreme,
> widely known as Lotus Born,
> with dakinis all around.
> I do practice as you did;
> please bring on your waves of splendor.
> GURU PEMA SIDDHI HUM

This is known as the seven line prayer to Guru Rinpoche, better known as Padmasambhava, the Lotus Born, born in Ogyan, commonly accepted to be located in the Swak Valley, the area where the Persian poet Jalaluddin Rumi was born, where the transmission of the Great Perfect originated, near the network of caves between Pakistan and Afghanistan today, where Osama bin Laden is even now holed up. Ironic isn't it?

Like Rumi, Padmasambhava teaches the path to liberation using symbols of desire. With Rumi there is a tavern where wine is served, where the grape skin of the ego breaks, and an intoxication begins. With Padmasambhava we have a celebratory feast and dancing dakinis.

The center of Tijuana's Revolución, where you risk being beheaded if you circulate your photo of the Three Graces, reminds me of the charnel ground, which in traditional Tibetan tantric mandalas is a sacred location—symbolically the landscape where you commit to things as they are, foul, frightening, a place of terror and anguish.

Sitting on mats of human skin
wearing ornaments of bone
drinking blood from skull caps
yogis and yoginis know the body
as both beautiful and full of decay

Peaceful, wrathful, ecstatic
elusive, yet with shapes
we are dreamlike and empty
pure, like the cloudless sky
this is the realm of Dakini

Nirvana can't be seen
beyond concept, radiant, clear
still, sentient beings suffer
since karma continues, although
the sublime is free and open

Dear Rychard,

As I told you earlier on the phone, do not worry about my heart. I am not waiting, you know, for Bouvard, who might linger forever hiding behind his indecisions, or his mysteries, whenever difficult emotions sully his midget nirvanas.

I shall go on and dance until the moon herself is tired. Kisses are my therapy and I shall have them whenever I choose. Bouvard is not the owner of my lips, and sometimes even my heart strays.

He stared at me, as he played,
as I stared at the passing lights,

kept to my figure eights,
snake arms and spins,
skirt and hair flying
against the neon martini glass.

His hands kept pounding on the dumbek,
Beledi, Saidi, Masmoudi rhythms.

Horns honked,
a cyclist almost crashed.
I could only hear
Bouvard's fickle heart.

Suddenly, I lost my balance; Alex
dropped his drum
and quieted the earth
with a kiss.

I thought no more of Bouvard
and his Dakinis in bikinis.

For one night, I was free.

From: Gabriela Anaya del Alma
To: Bouvard Pécuchet
Sent: Friday, September 22, 2006 4:59 PM
Subject: Re: disturbing news

Dear Bouvard,

All this talk of space, of being by not being, of floating, of celebrating that we exist in all things and yet we are nothing. But my body is no icon! And I am at peace in spite of my recent indiscretion, which I am quite sure Rychard did not reveal to you. Nor am I confessing, for I owe you nothing. I celebrated you with a kiss to a drummer. That kiss lasted longer than all of history. It was the tremor of creation and the end of everything. I was reborn and I died in those breaths we shared. I do not know his last name. I will not see him again. I am twice in love with you and longing for another stranger to appear in your place.

Go to your rock now, Sisyphus.

Anya

From: Bouvard Pécuchet
To: Gabriela Anaya del Alma
Sent: Friday, September 22, 2006 9:53 PM
Subject: size one tap pants

Even these rocks are aroused by your antics.
You bury my joy, but I have no trouble forgiving you,
and send the size one tap pants you requested.
I wonder if they will need coaxing.

If they could speak, the seat of the pants would complain
of being under the burning eye of your drummer.
O, I am sure they would like to fly open.
Ah, what terror would emerge!
Sometimes I think of that evening on the terrace,
the whiteness of your body in the moonlight,
and the whispered words of tenacious love that made
the trees tremble and the creek rush under the bridge.
Now I cry with operatic spasms over the earth.
I offer my neck to your swordsman.
Your divine feet, holy and just, tramp on my preciosity.
What could I say about flowers?

IV

SOUTH OF JACUMBA

SEPTEMBER 22ND–SEPTEMBER 28TH

From: Gabriela Anaya del Alma
To: Bouvard Pécuchet
Sent: Friday, September 22, 2006 10:08 PM
Subject: Tecate

Dear Bouvard,

I will be in Tecate for a few days, starting Sunday, to deliver and set up my photographs for an upcoming exhibit. My work will be shown for the first time in the country where I was born. I can invite four guests to the opening reception on Thursday, and I would like to invite you, Rychard, and Jampa, though I must warn you, Jacques will be there too. He is hell-bent on winning me back.

I took this photo of myself before I lost weight. Jacques said my breasts reminded him of the Willendorfian Venus, so he wrote this limerick:

> Was the wee Willendorfian Venus
> intended to woo us or wean us?
> Dry moderns may scorn,
> but this plump little porn
> surely tickled the primitive penis.

You could put your hands around my waist now. I wish you were here to carry me from the couch, where I often fall asleep, to my feather bed. I'm easy on your back, Bouvard, but hard on your conscience.

Will you come? Besos apacionados,

Anya

From:	Bouvard Pécuchet
To:	Gabriela Anaya del Alma
Sent:	Saturday, September 23, 2006 10:38 AM
Subject:	Re: Tecate

My dearest Anya,

Since early this morning I have been digging. There is a busted water line that runs from the gompa to the garden. The pipe is old, and the break is under a very important root of a very important tree, near some excitable monks who gather up every earthworm that emerges from my excavation and cover them with dirt. This concern for sentient life may seem excessive, but here on the side of this mountain, where the air is thin, the compassion thick, and the precepts strong, I am challenged to find a middle path between obsessiveness and a good fix.

I took a break, then, while the water subsided, and logged on to check my email, and found my last email to you rerouted back to me as an attachment to a wordless missive from yourself! Did I send this to myself as a forwarded email? Are you returning my letter unopened? The email that followed was an ad for penis enlargement, which somehow skipped through the firewall, a clever prong of marketing. Next came your invitation to attend the *Festival de la Cerveza* in Tecate and the advertised penis enlargement seemed in this sequence to refer to the limerick Jacques wrote, about how your breasts reminded him of the Willendorfian Venus, and ending with an image of a primitive prick.

The next email was from John Bennett, still recovering from surgery, containing another of his shards (a literary form he's developed that is a blend of prose poem and flash fiction) and explaining therein why he isn't going to continue to write shards. Since he had a near death experience, he...but this is all beside the point...what he wrote was that

People don't trust messages, although there was a time when queens wrote them in an elegant hand, sealed them in wax, and sent them hieing through the dark night on a thundering stallion, as often as not to be intercepted, the messenger shot through the heart with an arrow, the queen beheaded by a disgruntled king. The days of Western Union are over, thousands of hard-thighed young boys pumping bicycles through big-city traffic, messages tucked snug to their hearts: "Come home. Mother is dying." "Stay away. My husband has returned." "Sell the farm. Join me in Paris." "Abort. Repeat. Abort."

I really like the fuschia type, and this word he uses, *hieing*, good OE word, to hasten. Things definitely move along here. And the notice from you that Jacques will be there and John's "my husband has returned, sell the farm, join me in Paris." How far is Tecate from this copper-colored mountain? Should I leave my perch on this rock? That's Ekajati Peak, the breast-shaped mountain in the distance. Ekajati has one eye, one tooth and one tit, and I know if I start to explain the significance, you will wonder why I prefer one in the hand to two in the bush.

Two in the bush. Bush! Don't get me started.

Your servant,

Boo

From: Gabriela Anaya del Alma
To: Bouvard Pécuchet
Sent: Saturday, September 23, 2006 8:37 PM
Subject: Connections

All these connections, Boo, and yet our lips just can't meet. Tecate is just south of Jacumba, a place that is susceptible to fires, lots of dry foliage. Jacques plans to accompany me; I am always afraid to travel alone. He is not my husband; you know this. I do not feel obligated to resume where we left off just because he plans to make the trip with me. His company for my company, a fair trade. I feel sorry for him, but I can't limn a map to my heart. I do not even know the way myself, I only know when someone knocks.

Buenas Noches,

Anya

From: Bouvard Pécuchet
To: Gabriela Anaya del Alma
Sent: Sunday, September 24, 2006 9:32 AM
Subject: Re: Connections

Dearest Anya,

Beware of fires near Jacumba. This morning's Mo came up The Demon of the Heavenly Sun, NA RA, which augurs ill. The deceiver, a leader of wrong views, warns, "If the fire of desire blazes, oneself is burnt." But then, if this is an oracle, spoken by one with wrong views, how can I trust his advice?

And so, you travel with Jacques. Well, I am happy you are not traveling alone into such a brutal land. I know Jacques is not your husband; I can imagine what the vultures did to *that* carcass. But let Jacques be warned; I am making preparations to fly to your side. I am staying in the Poetry House and will soon finish my "Hymn to the Divine Feminine."

When I say *fly*, I mean I will do fast walking, a technique for travel taught me by Jampa Dorje, which is indeed a form of flying. The trick is to keep the feet close to the ground, so as to appear to be walking. Flying through the air is so *last year*.

As for Jacques, he had best carry his blade with him at all times. I am ferocious in a knife fight. I will expect him, or any other toad who insults or derides you, to meet me in the slaughterhouse yard on the outskirts of Tecate.

As for our lips, they will definitely meet. I have looked long enough at your photos. Looked until my eyes burned. I have ripped my eyeballs from their sockets, and four eyes have taken their place. I have also listened to your accusations that I was deaf to your desire, and tore my two ears from my head. I would tear the tongue from my mouth, but I have a better use for it. I could go on mutilating myself and recovering, but I have paid full price to clear up the past karma that led me away from your embrace. Now my mind is clear as crystal and my body filled with power. Yes, I know that in many ways I am still closed and inflexible, as macho as the next man, but I am determined not to lose you. Soon, my love, we will tango in Tecate.

Your soul mate,

Bouvard

Dear Bouvard,

I hope you are not on your way. I am writing you from home! I left Tecate two days ago. The trip was a fiasco. We had a flat tire on the way, and though we managed to arrive on time at the gallery to deliver my art, no one was there. I swore to cancel the whole exhibit, downed a third of a beer and split. I don't suffer any fool gladly, unless that fool kisses like you.

On the way home, as we waited in line for two hours to cross the US border, I realized I had forgotten the engagement ring Jacques gave me. I had taken it off to wash in the cantina bathroom. Yes, I kept wearing it, to fend off strangers, though really that ring never stopped you.

I've attached a photo of me in velvet pants. I haven't worn them since that time I saw you staring at me through the window at Claire de Lune, as I read my poems. At least, I imagined it was you. Was it? Why didn't you stay?

Come to San Diego. It's closer than Tecate. Please find a way to write or call and tell me where you are. I will 86 Jacques.

Confounded, yet alert,

Anya

Dear Bouvard,

Where are you? I was hoping you were coming to see me here in San Diego.
Jacques came by this morning to bring me a Starbuck's sticky bun and some coffee.
I thought I could give up sugar and caffeine, but it was too tempting. He gave me
a poem that he wrote to me the day I left him.

Yours,

Anya

Aubade

The sun is rising now, over
our little blue shack, and now reveals
the innocent translucence of your skin,
and all the pretty freckles you tried to hide.

There is another world of beauty underneath
your perfect form, beneath the still more perfect
power of your art. I feel it now
in the beating of your open heart.

I have told so many lies, to you,
and to myself, and all because
I did not want to hurt you. No—
I did not want to lose you, showing,

99

in too harsh a light, that underneath
this shoulder where you rest your cheek,
as I whisper poetry in your delicate ear,
is a wounded beast, rutting in the dark.

Why can't the sun stay put, just
for a little while longer, while its soft
morning light, and your soft cheek, smooth
the ragged, secret chambers of my heart?

But the day won't stop for me, or anyone.
Noon comes, dark falls, and every truth will out.
I am left, at last, with a familiar plea:
I love you. Forgive me. Come back to me.

From: Bouvard Pécuchet
To: Gabriela Anaya del Alma
Sent: Wednesday, September 27, 2006 8:42 PM
Subject: I last saw her in velvet pants

My Anya,

Where am I, you ask. I've been standing on a dung heap outside the slaughterhouse in Tecate; that's where I've been. I checked around, but found no trace of you or Jacques. What's up, I wondered. After some time, I found a cybercantina and checked my email. Ah, a flat tire, right, no exhibit, ok, that explains a lot; I knew I could be an asshole and complain I was stood up; however, I also was delayed. So, I'm sorry we won't tango in Tecate, but at least I got to see Ray Brown. Here's my story:

Fast walkin' my way to Tecate, I stopped in Berkeley to make a pit stop. I had a cup of tea north of campus and strolled over to the Doe Library to take a leak. Scrawled on the wall: "It's barbaric to be writing lyric poetry after Abu Ghraib!" Berkeley is still Berkeley, but now with a large number of orientals in the student body. T-shirts and Reeboks. The climate is more conservative than in the 60s, but Sproul Plaza still has its share of tables with petitions to sign.

On the Ave, I ran into Julia Vinograd, the Bubble Lady, selling her new book, *Dead People Laughing*. It had a photo of her on the cover sitting in the exact spot by the door by the Mediterranean Café where she was right then sitting, only she had on a different dress. Her dress that day was a checkered print. The dress on the cover of her book had skulls and crossbones.

I said, "Hi!" but she didn't recognize me. I said, "We used to hawk our books on the Ave in the old days." She still couldn't place me. "In the days of the *Peace and Gladness Anthology*, right after the Berkeley Poetry Conference in '65."

"Oh, those days. ancient history." I laughed and sat down and looked at her book. The first poem was titled, "For Moe Who Died." I'd been thinking of Moe, lately. I had recently had a chat with Hammond Guthrie, and he was glad I liked Moe; so many didn't.

"It's been a while," I said, and she agreed. I asked her, "Would you trade me one of your books for one of mine?" She was game, so I gave her a copy of *Chainclankers & Linoleum Nudes* with its three-color block prints of naked dancers. Julia's eyebrows rose, and she exclaimed, "Oh, my!" and tucked it into her shoulder bag. I bowed and kept on truckin'.

I realized I didn't have a lot of time to gab and sightsee. But at the corner, pasted to a telephone pole, I saw a poster for a gig that Ray Brown was playing at Yoshi's in Jack London Square. Ray is a jazz bassist. One of the greats. Born in 1926 into that magical generation of artists, he's played with all the famous big bands, with Diz, with the Duke and the Count. An *éminence grise*, he can still make that bass talk.

I made it down there at a quick pace and stood in line and drank cokes from the bar and watched the trains pass. I had a conversation with myself about life, love, and the pursuit of the perfect poem that goes, "Who gives a shit 'bout Agamemnon? Oh yes, we do, and we give praise to his skill in battle, homage to his lineage, and to the splendor of his armor. But I countered with, I think my true sympathy lies with Cassandra."

I only allowed myself time for one set with Ray Brown. Ray's sidemen are young guys, a black kid on drums, named Hawkings, and a white dude at the keyboard, named Geezer. Talented. But they had trouble staying in the groove. Ray, like a buddha, his big hands walking up and down the standing bass, shepherded them, gave them room to solo, and then marched them towards denouement and resolution. After the first set, I split.

I can remember the first time I left Oakland. It was after my dad told me not to show my sorry ass at his door, and I split for the Big Apple. Again, after I got a 0.9 grade point average for my year of free speech protest, and I regrouped in the seaside village of Aptos. Again, after my bust for redistribution of capitalist wealth, when I sold a copy of Macroeconomic Theory back to Cal Book Exchange without first buying it. Another time, after a jealous husband took my scalp but left my eyes, just for the glow.

Now, I was headed out one more time, after digging Ray Brown, en route to meet Jacques at the slaughterhouse in Tecate. I was cruising right along, when I noticed a sign that said Hillside, and I knew it should be bayside. When I got to an emblazoned Blockbuster Video, I asked a clerk how to get to the freeway heading south. She said, "I hardly ever leave Pinole." I wondered, where's Pinole? She asked if anyone knew about the freeways, and a dude in a stocking cap with an earring through his eyebrow stepped forward, and I knew that I was in a time warp.

Up the hill, the Parkway had four lanes with a street lamp every couple hundred yards, no cars, and everywhere outside the light was total darkness. One sign pointed left to the landfill, and one pointed right to the sanitation depot, so I kept going straight, humming a tune from Monk's *Mister Mysterioso*.

Around a bend, I encountered a hitchhiker, legs up to her ass, tight miniskirt, bare midriff, a tousle of hair and hip bent as she threw her whole body into a wave to hook a ride. In the distance I could see the glitter of the Chevron plant as I sped by, and I finally knew where I was, but I wondered if this maiden in distress knew where she was, and why she was where she was, and what my karma would be if I stopped for this dakini. But by then I was a long way down the trail, and she was a wispy memory, bright lit against the cyclone fence, and I was trying to figure out why I was headed north, when I wanted to be going south.

I turned around and made good time on the rest of my journey, but when I reached Tecate, well, you know the rest. If I harbored any ill feelings, they were totally dissolved by the vision of you in those velvet pants, which seems to go with a poem I had already written. Ah, my lost Lenore—

a girl in a car
    with a container of coffee in her lap
whispers she knows where Lenore is

she asked around
    questions direct and indirect
wondering if Hwy 10 goes to Alabama
    no, she didn't want to go to New Orleans
and she was told Lenore is in Baltimore

currently it's 93 degrees there
    humidity at 33 percent
wind from the northwest at 10 mph
    visibility unlimited

I remember her wearing velvet pants
respite and nepenthe from the memories of Lenore

If nowhere else, perhaps we'll meet, finally, in Paradise. I can never put my real feelings into words.

For now, I remain yours absolutely,

Bouvard

From: Gabriela Anaya del Alma
To: Bouvard Pécuchet
Sent: Thursday, September 28, 2006 9:37 AM
Subject: bastard bard

> Bouvard of my heart, Bouvard of the lost mountain,
> Bouvard, the bastard bard that I can't quit!
> You dare use jazz to excuse your dalliance?
> Do you think you've trapped fate by her fleshy thighs?
> And is it disappointment, or relief,
> to know you've never had me even once,
> keeping me, thus, both smug and unsatisfied?
> Perhaps one day you'll win my love, and see
> that I can only give my heart to reclaim it,
> while you, Bouvard, craving both sex and solace,
> pipe-dream a prelapsarian paradise,
> where you can sin, again, for the first time.

What has kept you from my bed? Surely not my decorous *no*? Did you hi-tail it deeper into Mexico? Are you in Cuernavaca, where I first cheated death at the age of four? My dear grandfather had a weekend house there. He warned me about the pond. But he never looked angry, hovering over my hospital bed.

We Are Made Mostly Of This

> Green pond of Cuernavaca,
> in you I begin to see
> my face. I imagine it
> gazed upon.

107

Your murky quality makes you
seem a jewel. I step in,
feel you chin-deep around me.

In the hospital bed, I hold
my rag doll loosely,
too sick from typhoid fever
to clutch,

too young yet
to mistrust water,

or comprehend
all that that implies.

Grandfather forgave me everything, even when in his giant library I reordered,
by color, his carefully arranged collection. A lot of busy work for a girl of five. I
had only that to do, or ride the green pedal car he bought me, up and down the
winding driveway until he arrived at night from work. He was the only father
I knew until I was six. Then my real father emerged and took me away to Fort
Worth. My grandfather died four months later, of sadness.

Ballad Of Gabi

Not long ago in *tierra Azteca*
Grandpa, sweet and savvy,
everyday sang slow *Mixteca*
and loved his little Gabi.

On every morning, sun or cloud,
he'd take her from the window
to where the marigolds would crowd,
and blue birds feed on Bimbo.

'Twas he who taught her how to read,
and he who held her up,
and he who kissed her tiny feet,
and he who held her cup.

But then her Dad came home from war
and said: "My Gabi dear,
I'm weary, so, of being poor.
No work for gringos here."

So off they went up north, although
dear Grandpa couldn't come.
And little Gabi missed him so
and felt so sad and glum.

"I'm so lonely here in Texas,"
Gabi wrote to him.
"Maybe he'll come home for Christmas,"
mom said, with a grin.

But then on Christmas Eve they heard
that Grandpapa had died;
And oh how Dad and Momma hurt!
And oh how Gabi cried!

So through the salty veil of tears
she wrote to Santa Claus:
"Won't you bring my Grandpa here
instead of all these toys?"

"They will come no more, / The old men with beautiful manners." I was his world.
I am obviously not yours; how then can you be mine? Nevertheless, I love you
enough that your absence stings. Explain yourself.

From: Bouvard Pécuchet
To: Gabriela Anaya del Alma
Sent: Thursday, September 28, 2006 11:15 AM
Subject: He went north looking for the chill in his bones

Yes, I see that I really stepped in it this time. Bad enough that I waited
for you on a dung heap. Now, I am deep in the same dung heap. Oh
well, there's enough shit to go around. I thought I would be in time for
the exhibition, thinking I would arrive fashionably late. Didn't expect
there not to be a show at all. I know I was truant, but Ray Brown was a
lot to pass up. At least, I didn't dally with the hitchhiker, and I felt I owed
it to Moe to commiserate with the Bubble Lady:

> Moe Macowitz was Jubal's bookselling guru. Moe's is a Berkeley
> institution. Moe Macowitz is dead, but his legacy remains. Moe's is
> still a great, great used bookstore, and is now run by Moe's daughter.
> Moe's and Cody's Bookstore and City Lights Books in North Beach
> were pioneers, the first to ride the tide of the paperback revolution in
> the late 50s and early 60s. The Cody's store on Telegraph Avenue has

recently shut its doors. I stood on the Ave and looked at the empty space. There was a poster hanging in the window which commemorated the great writers who had read at the store. Most of the Beats had read there, along with a host of mainstream writers. There was a photo gallery, and I laughed when I saw a picture of Bill Clinton next to one of Phil Whalen. They both had slightly surprised looks on their faces.

I was feeling nostalgic for the old days. It wasn't that long ago that I chatted with David Meltzer on the very spot where I was standing. Right behind me, on the corner of Haste and Telegraph, was where Lu Garcia and I had picked up Robert Duncan and spirited him off to Lu's pad in the hills. Once, I was standing on that corner, and I was hailed by Allen Ginsberg, who had just come out of Moe's. And just down the street from Moe's, I had argued with Richard Brautigan. "I don't buy books," he yelled, "I write books!" and stomped off. I don't what that was about.

Jubal had his first job as a bookseller working for Moe. And thanks to Moe's mentorship, Jubal started his own bookstore and coffee house in the state of Washington. You've heard me speak of The Four Winds. This was Jubal's livelihood for twenty years. He originally wanted to start a bookstore in Berkeley, and right after the Berkeley Poetry Conference, in 1965, he made plans to go to Alaska and make his fortune.

At the conference, he had the opportunity to confer with some of the poets in residence. Gary Snyder told him that Berkeley didn't need another bookstore, that Jubal should take what he knew about the Berkeley scene and find a place in the hinterlands which needed an infusion of culture. Jubal asked Allen Ginsberg if it was better to be a bad poet or a good business man. Allen told him, "Just be good," and Jubal took this to mean that he could be good at both.

Jubal's Alaska adventures followed, and eventually he and his second wife and a friend from Alaska, Sid Thomas, founded The Four Winds Bookstore and Cafe in Ellensburg, Washington. The original store was small. The three partners bought out a business called The Coffee

Conspiracy. This was in 1975. Starbucks had not yet gone public and was mainly a coffee roaster and wholesale distributor, selling their coffee to independent retailers.

The populace was new to gourmet coffee. On Jubal's first trip to Alaska, in 1965, he had stopped in Seattle to read a few poems in an open mic at The Last Exit on Brooklyn, a coffee house in the University District. They still served Folger's. No espresso bar in sight. No espresso bar in the whole city. In that era, there were only a handful of espresso bars in the San Francisco bay area, and the northwest was completely dry when it came to espresso. By the time Jubal settled in Washington in the early 70s, there were coffee houses springing up in Seattle, and Jubal remembered Gary's words and knew the time had come for him to put down roots and bring Berkeley culture to Ellensburg.

http://www.greatstreets.org/MainStreets/MainEllensburgHistory.html

The Coffee Conspiracy, then, became known as The Four Winds. The town needed new blood. It was a small cow town with a college that was voted one of the top ten party schools in the United States by Playboy Magazine in 1972. This estimation was based on the amount of beer consumed per capita. It was an ideal setting for a party town, as there were dance halls galore, left over from the glory days of the cattle drives of the last century, when Ellensburg, previously known as Robber's Roost, had been a major city, vying to be the capitol of the state. As it turned out, Olympia became the capitol, Walla Walla got a prison, and Ellensburg got a college—a normal school—to teach teachers in a high mountain valley, far from the temptations of the big city.

The 70s were a fertile time for change. The Vietnam Conflict was over, and here was a chance to relive the 60s revolution—sex, drugs and rock'n'roll—without the genocidal politics of war. The party began, and The Four Winds grew.

From: Gabriela Anaya del Alma
To: Bouvard Pécuchet
Sent: Thursday, September 28, 2006 12:24 PM
Subject: Beats, Books, and Coffee

Fascinating story, Bouvard. Once again you have attempted, almost successfully, to appeal to my predilection for excuses that involve beats, books, and coffee. Kiss me now and fuck off. Fuck Jubal; fuck Ginsberg, that ambiguous sage. You can't nurture wanderlust and love in the same novel and ask me to wait.

The only thing for me now is salsa music. Tonight I shall be deep in tropical rhythms. Salsa is like making love, which is why I gave it up, to be true to our future. You can't dance like Rodrigo. I know he still pines for me. I have heard he waits at El Torito Thursday thru Saturday for me to show up. He sips his Corona

113

and looks at his watch and doesn't dance with anybody, even though he can cut that Salsa rug like nobody's business. When the music starts all this will be over. To dance is to fly, Bouvard, to be unburdened and in love. I'll make sure to send a photo of me in my ruby dress. It is going to hurt, Bouvard. Go now and save your worms. You have respect for life, but not for love.

Indignant and Impervious,

Gabriela Anaya del Alma

From:	Gabriela Anaya del Alma
To:	Jacques Bâtard
Sent:	Thursday, September 28, 2006 2:08 PM
Subject:	Fwd: Beats, Books, and Coffee, and more

Dear Jacques,

I am writing off Bouvard. Not that this leaves an entrance for you. As you can see from the last email in my correspondence with him, which I have attached, I am going to salsa like I did in 2004, when you, desperately searching from club to club, found me at last in the arms of Rodrigo.

Thanks as well for the red dress you bought me last month, and for trying to appease me with ten different shades of red nail polish. None were exactly *chaotic*, but I appreciate the effort. Please come by and check on my dogs. I may not be home until morning.

I miss your kisses. How are your insects coming along?

Alma

Easy, my darling of darlings, I am aware I am amiss regaling you with stories and spinning gossamer threads. You are my Scheherazade, my true love, and you have every right to be frustrated by my absence and with my lack of sensitivity. You have been put upon by so many demands on your talents, and dealt real disappointments in real time, and then I add to your misery by failing to be early to my own funeral.

To be honest, I am not really sure I can go on challenging your various suitors and detractors: that toad who claimed he was a member of the Mexican mafia, that demented drummer at the cocktail lounge, that poetry critic (the very word *critic* sticks in my mouth; there is nothing baser) and now this salsa dancer, Rodrigo.

For me, there are no more stories to tell. I will make love to you the only way I can now, with words, long words, short words, dream words words of mutual feelings, a procession of words that move in you, a movement of words within you that reach your lips for a kiss. Think about this: words that visit you in the day, words that visit you at night, words that move in a silent way, words that search for your hidden fire, words that fill the bowl of your hunger, words that cradle you in their luminous blossoms, words that allow your flight to a multitude of worlds, words that tickle your goddess feet, words that nibble your goddess ear, words that are often lucky, words that in early morning help raise your spirit to meet the duties of the day, words that say they love your every way, words that say I shed tears for causing you distress.

I promise to shape up. My various projects have me by the proverbial balls, and you have me by the literal ones, or one, for that is all that remains after my horseback accident. I am not complaining. I had to limp those last miles to Tecate. Ah, my poor darling, what nights of rapture I owe you. I am the murderer of your transcendent bliss. Please believe me when I say I have deep feelings for our affair. I believe in our innocence. I do not wish to add upsetting reasons why I cannot reach El Torito in time to stab Rodrigo before his bestial hands touch that ruby dress. You will only laugh if I speak of the children. I swear that my only wish is to bring forth my very pure love. There is eternity in every second I am away from you.

Dear Bouvard,

Well, I can't very well go out now, can I? I am yours, my love, and that ruby dress shall sit in my closet until such time as you can take me out in grand style, and spin me until the moon is dizzy and drunk on our gazes.

I shall stay home, do Kegels, drink jasmine tea, and read the poems of our friend, Richard Denner. You know, I could have loved him if I had not met you. He presides over his universe of books like a mischievous god, smiling at the characters he has created for his own amusement.

Your sedated storm,

Anya

V

THIS RIDICULOUS CORRESPONDENCE

SEPTEMBER 28TH–OCTOBER 1ST

From:	Jacques Bâtard
To:	Rychard Artaud
Sent:	Thursday, September 28, 2006 10:12 PM
Subject:	This Ridiculous Correspondence

Rychard, be sure to give this to Bouvard. I will not condescend to write to him directly.

Jacques

> She confessed to me, at last—this ridiculous
> correspondence. I think she thought I cared, but she
> could no more leave me than her heart could leave
> her ribs, we are that tangled, she and I.
> I was a poet once, like you Bouvard,
> before I understood that the cold force
> of my imperious will alone could bend
> bones and steel as efficiently as words.
> And that was when I left you fools behind,
> with your paper castles, to ink my own epic
> in cum, powder, blood, and the Congo River.
> And now, after all I've seen, and after all
> I've done, this little skit is nothing more
> than children playing on Sunday afternoon.
> Children, poets, eunuchs, you're all the same!
> And when my little Alma is all through,

and crying with exhaustion, I will take her
into my time-scarred arms, scolding, mocking,
and comforting at once, until she sleeps
or weeps herself into oblivion.

From: Rychard Artaud
To: Jacques Bâtard
Sent: Friday, September 29, 2006 8:52 AM
Subject: whose spirit is this?

WHOSE SPIRIT IS THIS?

Ah, Jacques! Welcome. Glad you could join us.
Wondered when you'd show. Love the décor.
Love the hair. Sir Richard Burton on opium,
on the one thousand second night of translation.
Hoping you know the signs. A note of warning.
Circumambulate this mandala with care. A left-
handed path has its pitfalls. Tricky to traverse.
"Silly conversation?" Well, silly has its effect.
I see a softness around the eyes. Your hubris
is understandable, but here we do not suffer fools.
Gabriela is lucky to have your arms for succor,
and you well know Bouvard's not yet your match.
You may have wondered why he never shows up.
He's a golem created from fundamental elements,
a rat's foot, and a solution of hyposulfurous acid.
At this stage in his rebirth, he's only 9 inches tall.
Yes, he has the form of a little man, but he is
without internal organs, except for one testicle.
Amazing what can be accomplished with one ball,
but at 9 inches, he's only the size of a standard dildo,
though a dildo with four on the floor to be reckoned with.
Bouvard is the product of Tibetan and Talmudic magic.

Yogins and yoginis have perfected the rainbow body.
Here we are reversing the process and drawing benefit
by subjugating the gods and demons of the spirit world,
and training all the trainable beings to our materialistic ends.
You are a man of the world; and you should appreciate
these poets attempting to press their way into a velvet future.
Mr. Hecatone Stryix, do you or do you not believe in æsthetics?
Would you object if I smoked one of these perfumed cigarettes?
Love is stronger than fear, Jacques, and perhaps it is you who
have driven your mate to these excesses. She *is* a high priestess,
and her voice sings beyond the beauty of the sea, a cry not ours,
and any pilgrim would exclaim that this is a damn clever bunch.
There once were men with beautiful manners, but this time is past.

From: Jacques Bâtard
To: Rychard Artaud
Sent: Friday, September 29, 2006 10:12 AM
Subject: beautiful manners

I have received your letter, Artaud, though why I bother
answering you, or Jampa, or even that shrunken fool
Bouvard, who fancies himself my rival, this might clarify —
Even a bull, with blood-heavy sceptres of iron, and crown
of horn, still bothers to tail-whip pestering clouds of gnats!
And I'm glad you love the décor, and the feathery cap. I keep
forgetting how all these trappings may seem exotic, or comic,

perhaps, to those who know but glimpses of foreign manners
in moldering movies, or drug-addled visions of Marrakech.
But me, I have lived them, until I grew weary with them all,
like a housewife stuck in the suburbs. And nowhere was there sorcery;
nothing but ignorance—that and the man who knows a few tricks,
although I may just know a few more, Artaud, than you!
And as for that golem, Pécuchet, I may credit his power
much more than you might wager, for I have seen ironwood fetishes
polished and potent as he, and they seemed to glower with all
the reflected force that a thousand credulous eyes could lend them.
Still, they burned like trash when I tossed them into the fire.
Nor am I the vicious nabob that murderous rumor trumpets
(though sometimes it serves me well when fools will reckon me thus!).
You have noticed the softness around these eyes, which might be thought
to sparkle indulgently, while with child-like spells you ache
to fashion the slattern night in the shape of your velvet desires.
But do you imagine that they would willingly watch her leave me?
I love her, and love to indulge her, yes, and yes, I have learned,
through the bitterest wastes of passion, one cannot compel desire.
But do not forget what I have learned, as well—if we master
our own dark lusts, we will never again be scared of the dark.
You may call it my pride, my indifference, the strength of my own deep sadness,
but this black strength within me blooms with the power to choke,
along with my bruised affections, the cries of pity herself.
You tell me that love is stronger than fear? That is not my experience.
I suspect my Alma may yet be secure from whim, and from rival.

Gabriela Anaya del Alma
To: Harvey Goldner
Sent: Friday, September 29, 2006 9:08 AM
Subject: Bâtard, Bouvard

Dear Harvey,

Thank you so much for sending me the delightfully twisted *Dirty Old Man's Chinese Love Song*. I feel honored that you have dedicated it, retroactively, to me, and it was a pleasure to read it once again. After Rychard introduced you to me at the Mills College Conference, I googled you right away, and that poem is one of the first that came up.

I'm sorry I didn't get to know you better at that time, but you know how Bouvard loves to steal the moment, even if he doesn't quite know what to do with it. And now I need help, or perhaps some advice, or at least an objective opinion, and if all that fails, maybe you can reveal some secrets. You already knew Bouvard, and you mentioned in passing that you had also met Jacques. I was quite surprised at that, and I suspect I am not getting the entire picture. I have attached some correspondence for your perusal.

Yours in friendship,

Gabriela

Apparently you guys have a past! And Harvey has the lowdown on you both!

....

Forwarded Message

....

🌷 🌷 🌷 mi querida Gabriela:

Jesus, Gabby, ah sho duz worry bout you, you iz sooooo naheeeef. You trapped in a triangle wif 2 of th' mos fonee muthafuckas on the wes coast: Jack Bastard & Billy Beaver, aka Bouvard Pecuchet.. Jack used to work the Congo Room at Seattle's sleezyest transex strip/clip joint & the onlyest powder he ever knew werent no GUN, but Face. An he sho aint no Frog. Much less no Frog Poet. He did read a little Browning when he wuz in the kiddie reformatory at Waco, preparin fo a little skit "The Brownings" put on by Major Klamm, the perv who ran the joovie pen, and even then Jack starred as Elizabeff, not Robert. Billy Beaver was his cellie, his bunk/butt buddy. & ever since they hooked up again, back in '90, them 2 sleazeballs been rollin up & down hiway 101, preyin on innocent & lovely ladies such as your lovely & innocent self. But it really aint no problem, Gabby. Jus drop a dime on 'em to yr local sheriff or da FBI: Boff Jack & Billy gots outstandin warrants on 'em stretching from Sandy Ego to Wankoobah BC.

It's ME, miz Gabby, what RILLY luvs you. Once them 2 clowns iz back behind bars where they belongs, meet me in Mazatlan in the deep purple shadow of the Mango Tree.

 **H**

From: Rychard Artaud
To: Gabriela Anaya del Alma
Sent: Friday, September 29, 2006 3:25 PM
Subject: bouvard is angry and distraught

Harvey is murkily mixing desire with memory.
What he doesn't know is that butt buddies
hang together with more than a little patience.
He thinks he knows something about Bouvard
and Jacques. Sure, they did a stint in Waco,
way back in 64, but what about Waco 93?
How, after leaving behind, in the Davidian compound,
unrecognizable burned corpses, Jacques made his way
back up the Congo in pursuit of riches, while Bouvard
high-tailed it (interesting word) to Tibet?

It is not an exaggeration that Bouvard lacks substance
and that Jacques' imperious will can bend steel.
How do you think they managed the escape from Waco?
But to suppose you are trapped in a triangle is very
square, given the hypobolic nature of this affair. So,
go ahead and suck mangos with Harvey in Matzalan.
My sister married a mango sucker, and he was fucked.

Or we can move forward, turn the dull hyperbole
into a divine hypocycloid, with you the point,
rolling internally without slipping in our embrace.

From: Gabriela Anaya del Alma
To: Bouvard Pécuchet
Sent: Friday, September 29, 2006 4:55 PM
Subject: Re: bouvard is angry and distraught

Do not be angry that your secrets are not secrets to all, Bouvard. You always
hate to be found out. Harvey has reliable sources, though perhaps a need to
oversimplify our whole affair so that he may rescue me from both you and Jacques.
But perhaps I am the real terror in all this? If so, I'll take a bow and listen for your
applause.

It is true that you have made more obvious efforts for self-improvement, taking the
high road to Tibet while Jacques fed his lust for wealth and topless damsels in the
Congo. But in all fairness, Jacques does not have the luxury of Jampa's guidance.

And tell Rychard that he is wrong to turn this into a battle against fruit. Mangos are magnificent. Love is slippery and sweet even when it's bitter. Girls just want to have fun Bouvard, even girls who are poets.

Past The Black Door

When in a fit of fallacy
you are suddenly surreal, I am filled
with desire to believe
in your divinity—at times
lurid and indisposed—
drawing me past the
black door of dreams, beyond
the beaded entrance of your waking,

guided by a pentagram
poised unhidden in the sky—
all five points leading to desire,

constant as the purple-gold
nuclear moon outside my window
that asks for signatures in blood, the
blue basket of unassumed wanting.
I am so much—

you—
my own body wrapped in satin, enveloped
in an awful light.

What a shock it would be for you
to discover that I, soft
in your arms, am real terror,
deeper than sleep without dreaming,
fever and life, succubus,
your own hands
drenched in prayer oil.

131

From: Bouvard Pécuchet

To: Gabriela Anaya del Alma

Sent: Friday, September 29, 2006 6:01 PM

Subject: Re: bouvard is angry and distraught

I'm not angry about any exposure, and I am not angry with Jacques. My life is an open book. I need Jacques. You need Jacques. My anger occurs when an intruder misjudges our throbbing passions and our telling postures, and assaults, with insult, the temple of our making.

So, now you know Jacques and I have a past, several pasts actually, this past the fruit of our friendship in previous lives. It is rather strange for Harvey to pluck this one piece of past from the field of time. Bad Kabbala, in my opinion. In our geometry, the pentagram becomes the six-pointed star, which in turn is made from reversed triangles, male and female, in mystic union. Jampa has sent me to an unkempt Masonic graveyard on Elk Heights to mellow out. I have grown an inch taller during these last few exchanges, and I now have well-manicured finger and toenails.

On the horizon black clouds gather.

From: Gabriela Anaya del Alma

To: Bouvard Pécuchet

Sent: Friday, September 29, 2006 7:48 PM

Subject: Warning

Dear Bouvard,

I am sorry I have shaken you so by asking Harvey, the bold Seattle sage, to look into your business. I've forgotten how private you are. He only intruded because he wanted to help me and maybe help himself to the spoils of spilled secrets. Fortunately, I am too smart to succumb to his transparently seductive tactics. I suspected that this thing with you and Jacques was an old rivalry, but I had no idea the extent of your near misses and tomfoolery. I wonder if this is ever about me, at all. Am I a prize, a pawn, or a true love?

For now, I leave you to reconcile yourself with your past. I see how little I really know about you both. I will do my part and buy thirteen daisies. I will alternate between *I love Bouvard,* and *I love Jacques.* This worked for my mother, when she

chose my dad. She said it was the right decision, that flowers always know best. Well thank God for them, or I wouldn't be here to suffer you, or Jacques either.

WARNING!

Don't even entertain the impulse to challenge Jacques to a duel that you will surely lose. If the flowers have chosen you, then your death will be a pointless, cruel irony. In the unlikely event that you kill him instead, and he is the one the flowers have chosen, you will be disqualified. It happened to my mother's sister that way. The last petal decided that my Aunt Isabel actually loved Luis and not her other suitor, Adalberto. But that day, Adalberto, trying to undermine that ancient ritual, killed Luis at twenty paces. My aunt Isabel joined a convent and to this day brings thirteen daisies to Luis's grave every Monday, the day he died.

Be wise. Wait. Fate can be seduced, but she does not like to be questioned.

I love you, unless the daisies say otherwise. Until the last petal falls,

Anya

P.S.

The silk tap pants you sent have mysteriously disappeared. They were on my bed, still in the gift box, when I left. But when I got back home, though the box was there, the tap pants were gone and a single bloodstone lay in their place. I'm frightened, Boo. I don't think Jacques could have done it; he is out of town visiting Ruby, his stepmother, the woman who raised him after his mother died. He told me Ruby used to practice some sort of desert magic, but she has Alzheimer's now. I will not seek Harvey's counsel. You are irrationally jealous of him.

These *Roses of Crimson Fire* shall remain a secret shared only by our audience "fit though few."

From: Rychard Artaud
To: Gabriela Anaya del Alma
Sent: Friday, September 29, 2006 9:01 PM
Subject: on behalf of bouvard, mellowing out in the graveyard

Dear Gabriela,

You are neither a pawn nor a prize; you are love incarnate. Bouvard realizes this, and I am sure Jacques does, too. The storylike life you and Bouvard lead is in the great tradition of romance, and the feelings you and Bouvard feel are in the spirit of legend. You may pull his daisy in hopes of humoring him, but he only wants this war to die. Jampa says he saw Bouvard pulling out the pages of *Roses of Crimson Fire* one leaf after another, saying "Anya, Anya, Anya." This is becoming another poem on terror.

Bouvard is still in the graveyard, living under a tarp, doing penitence. He is learning impermanence. He may never come back. He knows the ruse of his being a golem backfired, and now he feels, at best, about one foot tall. He's a Scorpio. Indeed, he's a double Scorpio, with Mercury in Scorpio, so he's intense by half and needs his secrets.

Bouvard is undergoing an identity crisis, along with, it appears, the rest of humanity. The United States Senate thinks it necessary to disregard a thousand years of Common Law and dispense with Habeas Corpus for enemy combatants. Christian fundamentalists assail the Theory of Evolution. No Child Left Behind leaves all children behind. Astronomers decide that Pluto is not a planet.

And this last one is especially tough on Bouvard, because Pluto is the esoteric ruler of Scorpio. This fall, Scorpio is highlighted with up to six planets at one time occupying this sign of intense emotional transformation. For Scorpios there is a do-or-die mentality. Life is serious. When Pluto is afflicted (and being

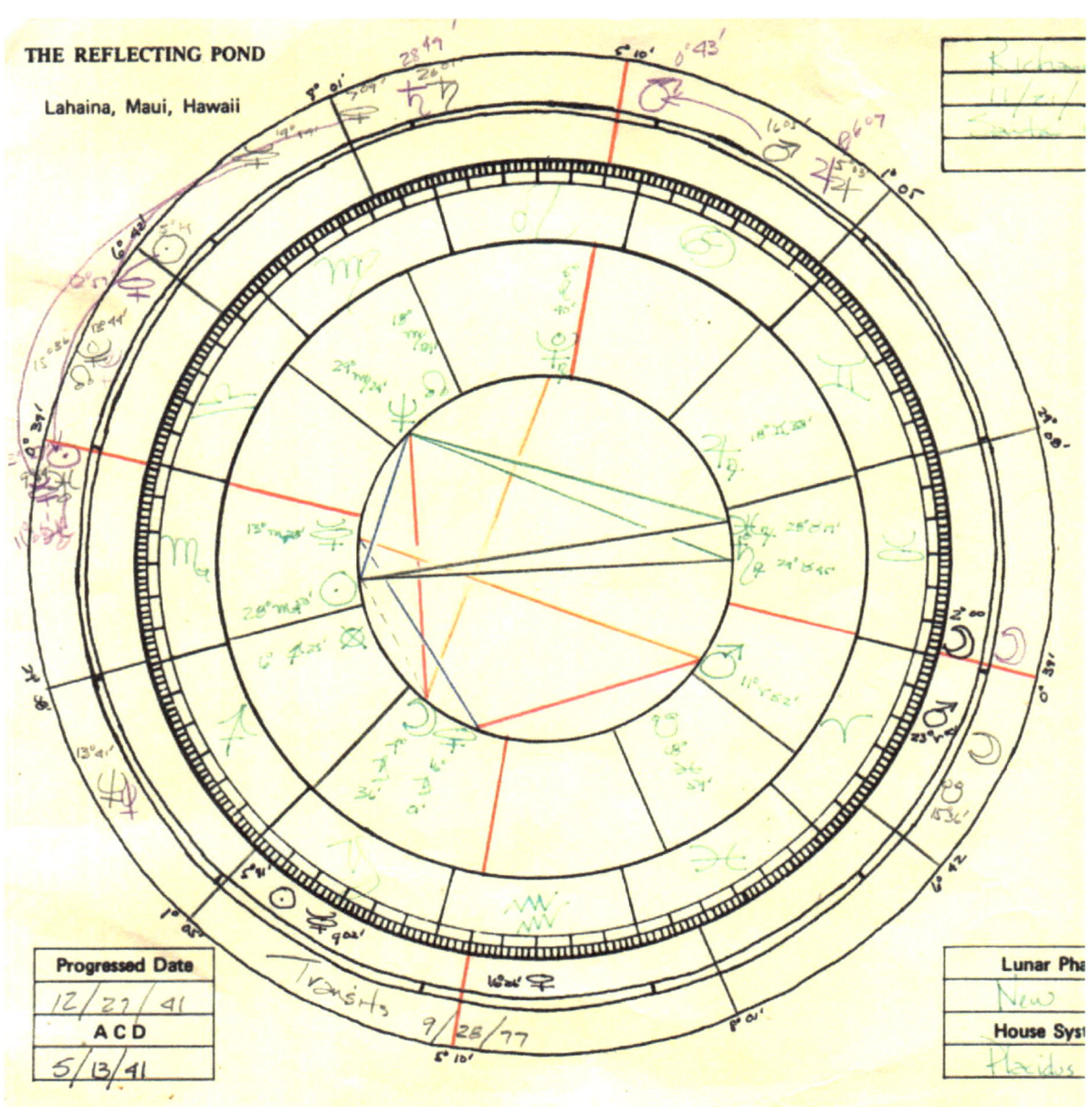

THE REFLECTING POND

Lahaina, Maui, Hawaii

Progressed Date
12/27/41
A C D
5/13/41

Transits 9/28/77

Lunar Pha
New
House Syst
Placidus

demoted to asteroid status might be construed as an affliction) the Scorpio native can suffer serious loss of faith as to whether or not there is any meaning to life.

On top of all this, the Autumnal Equinox features a solar eclipse in the early degrees of the constellation Virgo. Mars, the ruler of Scorpio, is particularly virulent when activated by an eclipse pattern, and Mars will be in Scorpio during most the season. Maybe Bouvard will pull out of his slump by the end of the year, but in the meantime, it looks like rough sailing.

i guess the next question is what happened to those size one tap pants, jacques probably took them with him to the desert to give to the shaman crone, as leonard cohen points out, a woman can still be attractive at 100 if she's wearing something tight

From: Gabriela Anaya del Alma
To: Rychard Artaud
Sent: Saturday, September 30, 2006 9:57 PM
Subject: Pillow Talk

Dear Rychard:

The daisy ritual will not be able to decide for me. The cross spells hovering over the graveyard where Bouvard is sulking have usurped the power of the daisies. Jacques would not like to be the winner by default. Well, yes he would. He doesn't care how he wins, only that he wins. Bouvard is my Phoenix, and Jacques, a man who shows weakness only to me.

Maybe my fate will be that of so many fictional women caught between two loves. When the writer can't decide who deserves her most, he kills her off. Oh the pride and passion of the gun, the impotence of our collective pen. As for the government, how can it be just when love itself is forever cruel?

And Love said, *if I have killed you*
where is the pulseless body?

I said, *I didn't know*
the writ of habeas corpus
applied to you.

I charge you with the
unconscionable act of
impregnating with hope
the deformed heart of a cynic,

of building highways
from my lips to
its rotting door.

Love, I asked, *how do you plead?*
Innocent, said Love,
no body, no crime.

P.S.

If you ever need a good pulvinosophist, Rychard, just put your lips together and blow. I give good pillow talk, the best in town.

Affectionately,

Gabriela

Dear Gabriela,

"Dear"—interesting term, from "deer," to stir up, to stir a hunter's instinct, as well as a term to calm the beast. The sun is out. Bouvard is probably glad that the rain has stopped. Some of the fog has lifted, if not in his heart, then at least in the graveyard of his mind, since Jampa continues to train our friend to reign in his thoughts. My guess is that Bouvard's willpower has evaporated. Nothing I can do about this, so I will leave them to their labors and turn my attention toward you. I appreciate your offer of pillow talk. I will try to oblige with what Jampa cannot and what Bouvard will not attempt, to give you satisfaction in body, mind and spirit. I hope you will forgive my businesslike manner. I proceed in all actions with a devotion to detail.

I begin my chaplet of song by addressing you as three separate beings in three separate guises, knowing full well you are one and the same in all forms. You are composed of a physical incarnation with a field of imagination and an indefinable energy that manifests within these totally adorable natures of body and mind. Virgin always. Mother of all blessings. Harlot, you are a natural woman.

If I were sitting on a bench and I viewed you walking down the street, my eyes would be drawn to the diaphanous creation of your energy. My appreciation would start with the mystery of your Botticellian feet, especially the ankle, the arch of the foot, the toes, the bones, muscles and joints that enable you to display such grace. I'd take in the shape of the digits and the soft hairs that rise from their sculptured poses. I'd look for sign of pit or discoloration and find each detail without blemish. Then, I'd look with psychic force deeper into the cushions between bone and fibrous tissue and here sense the frequent pulse of your blood's rush to feel the air. I know the blue of your blood is not the blues I experience when my eyes leave your visage. These deep blues are the aortic flow and pump of your inborn compassion. And if you looked my way, my eyes, discharging sparks of recognition of this loving kindness, would give halleluiah for the ankle connection and the toe tapping trap of longing that also allows me a look into your eyes for consolation.

And in the yogic calm of patience and the clarity of the yoga of diligence, I pray I may touch each public and private part of you, your skin, each follicle of hair, each breath of air and each liquid discharge of your chemistry through every exit and entrance, each face and orifice of your angelic carriage. They say angels are genderless. You, then, are unique and remarkable. The texture, temperature, color, and clarity of your skin gives information about your general and therefore your genital health. My gentility prevents any further mention of such a subject, but let me add that the epidermis, dermis and the subcutaneous tissues made from strong fibers form a dense bed perfectly made for my embrace. But dare I mention bed?

I'll continue my worship, although every direction I go puts me at risk. I'll begin with something small but tangible. The human, even in angelic form, is a hairy animal. Only the lips and palms and the soles of the feet are truly hairless. Each hair grows from a single follicle that has its roots in the subcutaneous tissue, and the follicle is nourished by the minerals, proteins, vitamins, fats and carbohydrates that you consume. O, lucky carbohydrates. As I was saying, the human, even in angelic form, is a hairy animal. Now, if the human were a bird, perhaps like the Greeks once thought (Aristotle categorized the human as a kind of plucked biped), we wouldn't need a bed for rest. We could hover or glide, sleeping on the wing, and when we mated, we could, in a flurry of feathers, find succor beyond the limits of our weight.

Mentioning weight is risky, I know. However, weight is a relative thing. Weight by its very nature shapes the body. Weight and gravity and a skeletal framework. Wait, lips play a part, too. Through my lips, my lungs below bellow a contrary force to weight. We can swim or soar beyond the confines of any statuary pose. Love moves us, and as I have written earlier, out there we walk on air in our new gravity. Out there. Out there. You are definitely out there, away from me, beyond my reach. Or another interpretation. You are out there, far out. Out of sight. Crazy. Cool. Hip.

So far, I've touched on skin and lips, hair, and now let me mention, if I may, hips. A judge begins with the ankles, sign of good breeding. The lover begins with the eyes, portals of the soul. The businessman begins with the hips. There is a movement within the movement, as she moves, that moves me in a way I cannot say. There's dancing, and then there is dirty dancing. Something in the style of moving. Something in the song of movement. Something in the movement of the light. Something in the tongue of flame that is evoked in the brain. Something that makes a tongue want to touch a clitoris and talk in buzz language. Much too quick, the tongue, but as the seed reaches for the sun by transforming moisture and warmth into a sprout, the throat senses the possibility of tasting nectar by the pattern of the buttock's play.

All this sounds a bit anatomical, mechanical, but on all of the levels that I adore you, spiritually, imaginatively, emotionally, with eros or agape, cellularly, molecularly and anatomically, a resonate string connects us, my sole to your sole, your soul to my soul, body to body, planet to planet, from this universe to universes beyond description, where it doesn't matter if big things get bigger or small things get smaller, my hands, even in the dark, know how to undo the belt of your robe and unfasten the clasp of the bloodstone necklace that dangles between your breasts.

Talk to me, my dove, talk, oh, nightingale, be the mockingbird of my passion, parrot my every touch, talk to me from along the downy pillow, talk to me in my dreams, talk to me at breakfast, lunch and tea. This dream talk is relief from the co-opted language of the political elite, succor from the linguistic stock and trade of everyday barter. Our words are like the luciferase enzyme in the

141

luminous organ of a firefly. If I pluck this light from one of these fireflies and placed it on your finger, would you engage me?

I do not want to be crude, and I will pose this in the guise of a Tantrik puja, a feast of divine nectars. Look at it like this: your lingua on my linga, my lingua on your labiam, locked in that location, we'd have a lifelong lifeline, and the lucubration of our literary effort would not only be lubricated by the latitude of this page but by the lavender laurels of our lavish language.

This is another poem about torture.

Rychard

From: Gabriela Anaya del Alma
To: Rychard Artaud
Sent: Sunday, October 01, 2006 3:28 PM
Subject: Re: Pillow Talk

Dear Rychard,

Nothing in this letter is true, or perhaps nothing in it is false. You decide: does fever illumine or does it lie? Your words have overshadowed, no nullified, everything that I have ever felt for Bouvard, or for Jacques, or even for Jampa. As I read your words I witnessed your own apotheosis, and was rendered myself, a woman of clay, something to be studied and viewed like a museum artifact. I am your factotum and your princess, your warmth and your distress. I weigh less everyday. I am heavy with longing.

Why do I feed Bouvard's dread for love? Oh, I cannot be his teacher! Why is Jacques so smug? He condescends with succor. And Jampa reminds me of

Pangloss, indefatigably hopeful; even as his syphilitic nose is rotting away, he encourages Candide to look to El Dorado.

I am pleading, and yet, I am walking away, disappearing into your garden:

The Pleading

Can I say to you stop trembling, stop terrorizing
the soul within the soul, tracing
the journey, buried in your eye's socket,

in the skeleton's memories, in the oboe
breathing, yet silent? Can you close
the stack of charmed books, the locket

with the picture of your misguided wish,
that caustic smile? If you stop now,
momentum will keep you afloat.

Within your tears is the force of water, within
your posture an effigy of Love's net; within your palm
the orchestra of the beautiful and the damned,

the naked, the undressed, the bald and the coifed.
Tomorrow speaks, now understands the past,
and yet the expectant moment hangs itself.

The heart lies hidden in bramble. I must ask to stop
saving. Say bonjour to your toes, hello to your spine, make it easy
on your chair, for it only wants to comfort you.

Everything you look for is in the layers of your mattress, in
your dark, impervious eyes, in the shifts of the wind, in
your sad and winding soul. Everything I see is you. I

am buried within you. Set me free to love us both. Set the sun
calmly onto self-destruction; it only wants to warm us now.
Like every waitress, it aspires to stardom. We must stand alone,

but in concert. We must put pennies in every spring, plant
in the winter and reap in summer. We must cultivate
the flowers that will line our tombs.

the celebration of uncertain futures
for you i burn, in you i breathe
what will i do when it's time to die?

From: Gabriela Anaya del Alma
To: Rychard Artaud
Sent: Sunday, October 01, 2006 6:41 PM
Subject: Re: bride and groom holding hands

As if hadn't fallen enough with your last letter,
now, Art, your art makes me crave
sex, wedding cake, and death.

I've come to regard Bouvard as an insect
and Jacques as a joke.

I'm entangled in your visuals, in your verbs, in your vowels,
which howled like I never heard from Ginsberg,
nor from the wolf of the Steppes,
who danced only to find out the pain of love
was worse than a gouty toe.

She vanished. He vanished. It was said
he was a model tenant, though no one wept for him.
I wake every day exhausted, after rummaging all night
for clues through his rented room, which smells
of dust, hope, booze, and betrayal.

Connections are impossible, but I will tell you this:
today I have lain feverish on my futon,

and Pancho has never left my side, not even for water,
though his tiny tongue is parched.

Please do not send more letters, (please
do not heed that request). I may be forced
to come to you, and my car has no brakes.

From:	Jampa Dorje
To:	Gabriela Anaya del Alma
Sent:	Sunday, October 01, 2006 10:33 PM
Subject:	Re: Multiple Universes: Beyond Definition

WHAT IS GOING ON HERE? I'm away, doing my best to prop up Bouvard's sagging ego, and now, what is that noise in my head? Is that the rumble of Rychard's id? Do I have to be everyone's superego?

I come through a ring of flames, which symbolize the transforming power of wisdom into one of the mandalas of Highest Tantra. At each corner of the grounds of the divine mansion there is a cemetery. Bouvard is in the one on the left. Here there are beasts of prey, which symbolize the dangers of illusion and the need to break away from uncertain pleasures. My yoga may not be enough to reverse the tendencies of you poets to incarnate into the five senses. However, Bouvard is making good progress in turning around the basic seat of consciousness. His graveyard meditation has made him realize that seeing everything in terms of I and mine, self and other, is a big mistake. This dualistic view has to buried or cremated in the charnel ground of his practice, and then the cemetery will be transformed into a garden of selflessness.

If you two, or three, or four, or five, or we six, can just hang on and keep from messing everything up, we can all go to the beach and have a picnic.

Thank you,

Jampa

P.S. Here is a play I found about you and Bouvard online at Unlikely Stories, www.unlikelystories.org:

The time is spring; the place, Berkeley. The Mediterranean Café on Telegraph Avenue. A woman and a man are seated at a square, marble table. He is a dandy. She is glossily beautiful, like a 40's sex movie star. They are in a pin-spot of light. Behind them looms a mural abounding with Greek gods and goddesses. They know each other really well.

BOUVARD: You are the embodiment of wild desire. You'd look great even in pajamas. If I'd met you first, I'd be with you, but I'm with her, and she's the best for me.

ALMA: She's the best for you? You've got to have an edge to love? I'm not good at loving with third-party people. Have I been here before?

BOUVARD: We get caught up in our feelings when acting with other actors.

ALMA: Leave it alone, Bouvard, the geography between us is a shield. Don't cut yourself off from wild desire. I've done it.

BOUVARD: I'm faithful to love, but it's not going to control me, just because all things have sex. It's torture to worry about us cheating.

ALMA: Too stressful, to be honest. Too stressful to be honest. I love this crush.

[She takes a drink from a tall latte.]

BOUVARD: Hard in this life, you've only one body.

ALMA: Only one flag, only one life, only one leaf. Good line, Bouvard.

BOUVARD: I want to coddle...I mean cuddle you, well, both, but I know you have a natural feminine, non-toxic, body-pure immunity to adultery.

ALMA: You're right, I am careful about hygiene. It's a thing with me, but [*unctuously*] if I was to be unfaithful, it would be with you.

BOUVARD: You, you, you…at least, you're not dumb. Blind, maybe, but not dumb.

[*He takes a sip from her glass.*]

ALMA: True love's an exotic club, that's for sure, and we've got the talent for it.

BOUVARD: [*He rises.*] True love is just a romantic notion.

[*She finishes the drink.*]

ALMA: Keep it up.

BOUVARD: Do you give heart? [*His line overlaps hers.*]

ALMA: I struggle to keep house. I do everything but cook. I can spend the whole day reading in bed. No reason to find someone else, besides me.

BOUVARD: And people have everything, including self-sabotage. [*He sits.*]

ALMA: Why are you fidgeting?

BOUVARD: [*straightening himself in his chair*] My pants are too tight in the crotch.

ALMA: If I had to choose between my survival and my dignity, I'd choose love.

BOUVARD: [*wistfully*] Yes, I miss the hungry years—but not too much. Then, you don't have time for love?

ALMA: No, but you encourage my wild side. [*half rising with excitement*] There's a charm in love affairs. Fun to be with you. Pure passion. Endless. Reckless.

BOUVARD: A kiss from you couldn't hurt, babe.

ALMA: With kisses come consequences. [*slumps*]

BOUVARD: I know you could cook my perfect omelet, too.

ALMA: [*ignoring him*] Once, I went on a date with a guy. Walked on the beach. I kissed him, but he didn't call. Wished he had. I took my blouse off. Had on a plaid skirt and boots. Took off one boot because he wanted to see if I had cankles.

BOUVARD: *Cankles?*

ALMA: He wanted to see if he could tell where my calves left off and my ankles began. I knew he didn't have balls.

BOUVARD: And I'm playing the part of a…I just feel intoxicated by my desire for you. I could kiss you all night. [*nonchalant*] Just a physical fact.

ALMA: [*She puts both gloved hands over her ears.*] I can't hear a thing you're saying.

BOUVARD: It's nothing, but all the same, a kiss from you couldn't hurt, babe.

Dim lights. Sparks fly.

VI

A FAMILIAR FEVER

OCTOBER 1ST–OCTOBER 12TH

From: Jacques Bâtard
To: Rychard Artaud
Sent: Sunday, October 01, 2006 11:53 PM
Subject: Quis custodiet ipsos custodes?

Artaud,

My desert ceremonies have just been interrupted by a very interesting
call from Alma. I was inspired to write the following:

> My mother is a withered crone,
> my father a professor,
> but both agree, a toad's a toad,
> and lower is the lesser.
>
> We spend our little lives
> running from our teachers,
> and after all our errantry
> come back to our own nature,
>
> where some, on deserts of the mind,
> waste their shriveled seed,
> and others father history
> in ogasms, and blood.
>
> Some were born for *eros*,
> some born to indecision;
> some were born for treachery,
> some born to be the hangman.

155

Dear girl, come inside and close the door.
Come in, but understand, you can't marry me.
I'm already married to Eleanor Rigby.
She just loves weddings and has a house full of rice
she's picked up at other people's weddings.
I couldn't resist her, and I was right to marry her.
Now, I'll never be lonely or hungry.

You can't marry me. I'm a high plains drifter.
Eleanor is back at home darning my socks.
It's mainly me and my horse, Patches.

156

That's Eleanor with me on Patches, that curly blond girl.
And the little man behind the telephone pole, that's the preacher.
Again, us in front of our new Cadillac on Donner's Pass.
Our grandparents were survivors of the party.
Not so, one of our cousins.

Yes, I'll take you to bed, but you'd be better off waiting for Bouvard.
He may twist and turn like a snake in hot water trying not to commit,
but once Bouvard sorts it out, he'd make the better mate.
You need a man who's not slippery and lightnin' quick to flee.
Besides, I enjoy playing in the orchestra of the damned;
my great-great-great-great grandfather invented the clarinet.
Forget marrying me, unless you want a bundle of blues.
So, now, how'd you like to hear my version of *Sophisticated Lady*?

From: Gabriela Anaya del Alma
To: Rychard Artaud
Sent: Monday, October 02, 2006 5:29 PM
Subject: Re: but you can't marry me

Lothario!

I now see you bring a woman to the edge of terror and delight only to push her off. Marry you? You wish, Artaud, you wish. I wouldn't even kiss you now, even with Bouvard's tiny, cursed lips.

And I like to kiss, Artaud, especially when I've tasted a good scotch. I'll kiss everyone at George's on the Cove, but you. And I'll never be drunk enough to fall for your prickish prose. Have fun with Eleanor. I hope she chokes you with her ragged stocking. Leave me to my flu; I'd much prefer it to your version of Bob Dylan's *It Ain't Me Babe*.

As if *I* would beg *you*! It is you who will learn the futility of begging. You have more words than heart. You're as shallow as the holes my chihuahua digs to bury his bones.

Artaud, you blow!

From: Rychard Artaud
To: Gabriela Anaya del Alma
Sent: Monday, October 02, 2006 7:26 PM
Subject: Re: Lothario

Lothario! That's a low blow. That shot will be heard around the globe. Did you check out the Wikipedia entry: http://en.wikipedia.org/wiki/Lothario? That

158

Dylanesque ditty was definitely not the proper response to your passionate appraisal of my art. I should never have tried to put you on about being married to Eleanor Rigby. Now, I feel like another Beatle's character: Maxwell with his silver hammer. Only this time I hit myself on the head.

I've been watching too many existential westerns. High plains drifter, indeed. High on plain old hokum is more likely. Just plain pathetic, that's me. If I had known you were weak with fever, I would never have strummed that ludicrous melody. I thought you had thrown yourself down on the ground at my door as a bit of drama. So, I fell into the stereotypical role of an untouchable bad boy.

By the way, that little blond girl in the photo is not my wife, silly. She's my sister. We were much to small to drive such a big car. That is, however, a picture of my faithful horse, Patches. And the fellow by the pole, my friend Neil, did become a Catholic priest. He was secretly in love with Lynda, and there was a popular song in those days that celebrated someone with her name. Neil had an old 78, which he played until it was so scratchy that it sounded like a mouse eating crackers.

I remember another song from those days: *Open the Door, Rychard*. Now, my only wish is that I had been quicker to open the door and help you up. Please forgive me.

Your humble servant,

Rychard

From: Gabriela Anaya del Alma
To: Rychard Artaud
Sent: Monday, October 02, 2006 9:07 PM
Subject: Re: Lothario

I cannot take any more tonight, Artaud! How quickly your tone changes from letter to letter. A true lady would never propose to you, or to any man. My mother raised me well, telling me "La mujer debe de ser rogada no rogona."

Bouvard is a sentimental little boy; Jacques is a deluded patrician; you have the words of Cyrano, without his character. I am not a player in your play. God and Lucifer will share a kiss before my lips will touch your pillow.

Good Day, Sir!

Gabriela Anaya del Alma

From: Jampa Dorje
To: Gabriela Anaya del Alma
Sent: Tuesday, October 03, 2006 7:26 AM
Subject: Re: Lothario

Dear Miss Gabriela,

Right from the start, this morning, I knew things were askew. My Word program opened with the warning that changes had been made to the global template. I knew immediately that this computer had been tampered with. I sensed, by the sulfurous smell, that it was Artaud, and that he was paying us a visit, unannounced.

I had spent all night in the graveyard helping Bouvard perfect the yogic sadhana known as the Reversed Padmasambhava Lotus Pose. In other words, he has been standing on his head, supported by his arms in tight formation around his head, with his legs in a full lotus, atop a gravestone. This position may sound uncomfortable, but it is the best thing to increase beneficial prana and alter the neurological pathways in the bad brain of a frigid procrastinator like Bouvard. He needs to thaw out and get some hot steel in his spine.

The fog of false dawn still caressed the tombstones on the plain, when Artaud burst through the ring of fire on the perimeter, singing some of his silly doggerel. He's so sarcastic. If I was not as even-tempered as I am, I'd slap him silly. The song went something like this:

> Om Om in the graveyard
> Where the ghouls and hungry ghosts roam
> Where seldom is heard a compassionate word
> And the yogis all sit on their bums

You nailed him perfectly with your comparison to Cyrano de Bergerac, but I think his nose is growing even longer than dear Cyrano's, and I would compare it to Pinocchio's. Artaud is a wooden-headed dumbkoff for treating you the way he did. And you, my dear, are a wise woman to stiff him. Just the idea that he pulled the welcome mat out from under your feet as you approached his door makes me seethe with anger, and it is only because I can spontaneously liberate this anger as it arises, that I didn't take a stick to him.

When the fog lifted somewhat, this wretch saw Bouvard and I from a distance. He had the good sense to prostrate himself, and I could tell by his style that he has been properly trained; otherwise I would never have consented to an interview with him. I must admit, as obnoxious as he can be at times (those songs of his, my god!), he can be charming when he desires to be. Yet, there is something schizophrenic about his behavior. He is syrupy sweet, almost to the point of glue, and then he shifts into his salty dog routine. Bouvard, on the other hand, is a classic psychiatric case of manic depression. If I were to put these two together, we'd have a behavior called schizophrenic non-decisiveness. One for the books.

All the same, I was impressed by Artaud's contrition, and his willingness to undergo training, but I still have doubts as to his motivation. I will put him on probationary status. Set up a regimen of purification. See what comes of it. I can't believe he is serious when he says that he innocently believed he was doing an Apache Dance with you. I wasn't sure at first what this referred to. Monks don't dance profane dances. I admit, as a youth, I was a foxy dancer, but this was before the days of Rock 'n' Roll, when Swing was the thing. Anyway, I was curious about this Apache Dance thing, so I did a bit of research. Check out these links, if you will:

http://www.eijkhout.net/rad/dance_specific/apache1.html

http://en.wikipedia.org/wiki/Apache_(dance)

Sounds to me like a page right out of our Artaud's namesake's Theater of Cruelty. I hope when Rychard read the admonition, "We cannot go on prostituting the idea of theater whose only value is in its excruciating, magical relation to reality and danger," that he did not believe he had to take real physical actions against your sensibilities. If this is so, I fear we have gone a lot further down the road of torture that is the order of the day than I imagined. To think that there are still 300 years left of this Kali Yuga Age. As for now, about the best Artaud can hope for at this stage of his development is to be reborn as a bacterium on a septic tank.

What Artaud needs is a good dose of The Theater of Purification. I have decided that a stretch of dark retreat will do wonders and have sent him off to Mine Shaft #4 where he can deconstruct his present view of reality. This is the mineshaft where the bodies of the Chinese miners were interred, so Artaud will have good company.

As for you, my friend, I think it best you try to relax and attend to domestic matters. Quiet is the key to healing. I will check in on you. If it still matters to you, Bouvard is progressing nicely. He has grown a lot in his time here. He's now well over five feet. His hair is coming in nicely. Internal organs are mostly complete. Still working on his heart. The heart is tricky, as you know, but I think a seamless fusion of 50s cool jazz and moonlight will do the trick.

Yours, as ever,

Jampa.

163

From: Gabriela Anaya del Alma
To: Jampa Dorje
Sent: Tuesday, October 03, 2006 9:07 PM
Subject: I'm a kissing girl

Dear Jampa,

I'm always uneasy corresponding with you. because while I'm an iconoclast and a kissing girl, your manner seems ever endearing and fresh. No matter. I will trust in your resolve.

I revolt against the Apache dance! How vile of Artaud to think of me in such a way. I would never be his whore, or even pretend to be his bitch. No! If anything, he would drink wine from my shoes and record the poetry I murmur in my sleep. That's how it would go between Artaud and me. The delusional fool!

And to think I have thought of Artaud as a passionate friend since the moment I met him at Mills College, just a few short weeks ago, after I sneaked down from my dorm room in my pajamas to snatch a bite from the closed kitchen. Just as I snagged a remaining blueberry muffin, I turned around to see Artaud staring wildly, and yet seeming to be completely in control. He escorted me to the dusty library and sat and looked into my thieving eyes, while helping himself to my baked goods booty. We exchanged only a few words. He put his arm around the small of my waist and walked me to the foot of the stairs. I turned around to thank him, for what I'm not sure, and he gave me a soft and lingering kiss. It could have become passionate and wet, but it didn't. There was so much sex in our restraint.

But that was the only time he touched me. And he looked quite stone faced, the next morning, when he told me that he was an old acquaintance of Jacques! Still, I felt our friendship would outlast his habitual, five-second affairs with tart after tart. I even felt as if he might become a kind of secret society, continually watching over

me, while all those who seek to do me harm fade into irrelevance. Even Jacques, who acts so confident in the face of any rival, squirms at the name *Artaud*.

And then suddenly, just when I began to mourn Bouvard, resigning myself to the fact that he has only ever been, at best, a tantalizing ghost, I get this love letter from Artaud, claiming that all my geography, from head to toe, is somehow bound to the ventricles of his heart, to the nerves in his fingers, to his frontal cortex, to his foreskin, to the part of the brain that dreams!

It was only natural that I entertained the idea that Artaud had come back to court. I imagined more kisses like the first, long dinners in the veranda, and shared evenings watching bad movies that would make us laugh and curse Hollywood even more than we already do. But now I see, not the passionate friend who penned the most beautiful prose I have ever read, but a cruel and empty man. A snake of a man, a scoundrel, a smarmy playboy, and with bad taste in art besides! Artaud, the man-ho. I think you will agree; he must be reborn a thousand times before ever getting back to the beginning, before I saw him revealed as the ugly cock:

> The ugly cock gets a lot of play,
> in spite of his ear contorting call,
> wobbly walk, and dirty feathers,
> simply by virtue of
> his accidental monopoly.
>
> And the hens never bother to look
> for a better, beyond the pen.
> They are convinced he
> is the only cock on the lot.
> And the cock couldn't be happier.

Dear Miss Gabriela,

I understand your uneasiness when writing to me. I know our relationship might be misinterpreted by people with vulgar minds or by those with official responsibilities in maintaining order, but under the present circumstances, I cannot see any way around our situation.

I now have two charges: first, Bouvard (remember him?), and then there's the derelict, Rychard, who squirms under the pressures of the purification practices to which I have set him. His residence in the deep confines of a mine shaft in the side of the Copper-colored Mountain is only a start in the decathlon of rehabilitation he must finish, if he is to have any chance of purgation. He will remain in the dark, and I will take him supplies and place them in an outer chamber, where he can retrieve them after I have resealed a set of panels I have made, so that no sunlight can reach him, and he will come to see the clear light of his spontaneously arising pure nature. I know his guilty mind struggles to make amends, because this morning I found, scribbled with charcoal on a brown paper bag which I had used to bundle his food, a series of *dowa*, or poems of realization, that are addressed to you. My advice to you is not to make much of them. They are clever, but, for all his talent, his wit will not supplant his need for wisdom. Here they are.

> There came a beam of soft light
> from the bottom of a mine shaft.
> This is a shaft of my own making.

A shaft that is totally mine,
I am buried deep in the visible.

And now, there's a flow of sweet honey
seeping from the walls of a well.
This is a well of my own making.
A bee building a cell in a well,
I am buried deep in the visible.

I make with my mouth a speech
that confesses to you whom I love.
This is a mess of my own making.
A hole in the sole of an old shoe,
I am buried deep in the visible.

Upon your head you wear a crown of stars,
stars that guide me in the night of my soul.
This is a darkness of my own making.
All the tortures of hell overtake me.
I am buried deep in the visible.

I try to surround you with these words
that I hammer to sludge with a sledge.
These words are rocks of my own making.
A blind poet who follows a blind muse,
I am buried deep in the visible.

I deconstruct the *w* in the word *word*
until a pit in the mountain breaks open.
Therein is a woe of my own I am making.
A half-naked temptress floats above a monk,
and I am buried deep in the visible.

The hare Buddha rewarded and sent to the moon
pounds the ingredients that make the elixir of life.
With pure devotion, it is a new life I am making.
Gabriela, don't let me fall back without hope;
please smile on this wretch buried in the visible.

From: Gabriela Anaya del Alma
To: Jampa Dorje
Sent: Thursday, October 05, 2006 5:00 PM
Subject: Espionage

Dear Jampa,

I am grateful; had you not prefaced the poem with your admonition, I may have given Artaud a second look through the peep hole. How wretched to be so skillful with a pen and so utterly lacking a talent for love.

I am to dance tonight, but not at the regular club where my naked breasts shimmer from a tall stage. No, tonight, I am Zephyr in coin bra and sequins at a raw food restaurant and club by the sea: http://neshamaraw.com/.

In spite of what I swore to Bouvard, I shall indeed cross paths with Alex again. Tonight he is, once again, my drummer, lord of my hips. I shall keep to my course and not stray, reminding myself that I am, forever, a spy in the house of love.

Dear Spy,

You were dancing at a raw foods restaurant, and there were dancers outside the Four Winds. I was stretched thin, what with Bouvard and Artaud in their locations and me flying from the graveyard to the mineshaft to the corner of Fourth and Pine. I did not mention to Bouvard your dancing to the drums of Alex. To be honest, I don't think it would faze him, but I thought I would remain discreet on this subject. You would be proud of our Bouvard, as of late. Jealousy is not one of his weaknesses, now, nor anger. Ignorance, yes, but two of the three driving forces of his karma are burning with much lower octane. Recently, he has been building mandala sculptures with found objects that he finds on his way to visit me at the stupa where I do my circumambulations.

Your continued interest in Artaud is interesting. I am glad your anger has subsided somewhat. I am sure you are still in a defensive mode, but I know you do not want to carry your tiff with your friend too far. It is good that he has been chastised, but we must leave a ray of hope, so Artaud can find the path.

Your reference to *A Spy in the House of Love* is of course apt. Do you remember the story Anais Nin relates of her meeting with Antonin Artaud at the Sorbonne? He had been invited to the university to give a lecture. His subject was *The Theater and the Plague*. He delivered his lecture to a full house. He began with a history of the plague. Next, he described the physical symptoms in graphic detail. His thesis was that the plague had reached such a level of apocalyptic proportion that society was pushed to extremes, and that this impending doom drove artists to work at fever pitch to produce great works. His words were scintillating. The rhythm of his delivery fused with the psychological discomfort he was relating. He portrayed the crazed bodily fluids that flood through the body of the victim of plague. The audience became alarmed by the magnetic suction of Artaud's presentation. It was as if black bile was gushing from between his teeth. He fell to the floor and began to thrash his limbs and twist his torso in agonizing contortions. Then, the audience began to pulse in discomfort. Artaud continued his revolting display of bubonic bathos. People got up from their seats in revulsion and fled the auditorium until there was none left but sweet Anais, sitting in the front row. Artaud rose from the floor of the stage, came down the steps, took her hand, kissed it tenderly, and invited her to join him for coffee at a nearby cafe.

I am not sure you are ready, however, to join our Artaud for a social visit. I do not recommend you peeking through any peephole. He must remain sealed in his cell until there is a shift in his sensibilities. Meanwhile, I continue my work on these rascals. I hope to present them both to you as a pair, once I have completed my refurbishing. I plan to oversee all aspects of their recreation down to the final detailing.

My work is monumental. Never have I created such masterpieces. A pair of obedient servants to fulfill your every wish, they will please you to no end once I am finished with them. They will act as bodyguards, as footmen, as guides, as whatever you wish, and they will come with a trial test option that will last one complete moon cycle, so you can get the feel of them, and if you accept them, there will be a full warranty. Bring them in anytime for a free lube job and tantric tune-up. Remember our motto:

Wheel your rig into DICK'S.
You'll get a square deal.
Dick distributes Punch Products.
Punch protects your transmission
parts. Perfect parts
produce the proper frequency
to transcend planetary interference.
Pour Punch in your crankcase; it'll become
a peacock with 6 heads and 9 tails.
After this rite, things will be right on.
Stick it in your gas; it will swell
until there's a tyger in your tank.
Stuff it in that stash behind the dash.
Rub it on your hood or slip it in your ear,
Punch stops heat, sludge, jerking
and the formation of calluses
on your eyes.

Dear Jampa,

I am suspicious of any man who claims to have conquered jealousy. If Bouvard is telling the truth, he has become a man without passion; if he is lying, his jealousy is poison. I only trust men who will not speak of it, whether they have it or not.

Jacques, at least, has no pretense in this regard, despite his arrogance. His eyes were still wild with the desert when he burst into the restaurant last night. I didn't know quite how to react when he grabbed the tip basket, stared at Alex, and whispered, *Pompeii, Pompeii.*

I fear that these Stepford Wives you are making of Bouvard and Artaud will not suit me at all. Perhaps you are trying to fashion them after the men in my poem:

Goddess

Perhaps they were touched
by something
I said in passing,
some careless glance I could easily
have given a bird or
an attractive handbag.
Now they are spiders
tangled in my hair,
harem men

174

who resemble Valentino,
who drink
wine from my shoes, record
the poetry I murmur in my sleep.
They feast
on my laughter, bring me
grapes and cider,
massage
cucumber and melon oil into my skin.
They whisper sentences with the
word *forever* into my neck.
I am their *joie de vivre*,
adored beyond
sex.
I say to them:
Show me your
perfect penises,
pretty men
all in a row.
Give me your beautiful teeth
your hearts of gelatin.
Light my candles.
Be drunk on my drunkenness,

drunk as fools
have never been.
Say things kings so often don't say.
Do you want
sugar in your tea?
Shall I swat a bumble bee, or whatever
small thing might annoy?
They had better never
ask me to choose,
ask me to say things
women too often say:
I'll mend your socks,
have your baby.
I'll cook you breakfast.
I need.
I love.
I'll never lie

with so many like you, giddy,
on a bed that exceeds
the span of God's
very large wings.

From: Jampa Dorje
To: Gabriela Anaya del Alma
Sent: Friday, October 06, 2006 9:06 PM
Subject: Re: Goddess

Dear Miss Gabriela,

Goodness gracious, not *Stepford Wives!* Think *Blade Runner* and *Matrix Reloaded.* I do not believe I can expand further than God's wings, but I do know that Rychard is tuned up, topped off, and running smoothly. Bouvard is mostly silent, but he runs on mantras, and his OM meter reaches up to 100 bhumis. So, he is good on the tight curves and also over the long haul.

He never said a word about jealousy, by the way. It was not he that mentioned the word but I. I had planned to present both Bouvard and Rychard in tandem, but my calculations on Rychard's progress were quite a bit off, and since I was pleasantly surprised at Bouvard's attainments, I feel I should offer him to you now. Realize that I had to reduce him to basic elements and reconstitute him using a very experimental process of vajra demon subduing; but it seems to have worked, and so we have a new Bouvard. I am confident you will find this Bouvard more in tune with the Meaning of Love and the Means of Love, ready to please you in whatever capacity you wish.

I have only one reservation. In the reconstitution of his heart stream, I only had one music program, which I had to share with Rychard, so I used the Classical to Romantic tradition for Bouvard and the Post-romantic to post-modern section for Rychard. This means that Bouvard will only be able to dance up to and including the merengue. His waltz is quite amazing. Rychard will be able to foxtrot, bebop, swing, twist, and do post-modern dances like The Net. Be cautious at first; Bouvard has a tendency to overheat when he tangos. This is because he feels the dance is far too macho, and it builds up pressure in his misogyny compartment. If you try the tango, let him let you lead some of the time. Otherwise, he is 100%.

I have attached an invoice for your records. Please print out, sign the release, and return a signed copy to me. Of course, there is no charge. May you enjoy your time together.

OLD LOVER REFURBISHING

Service Department Hours 7:30 AM to 5:30 PM

CLIENT: BOUVARD PECUCHET

Vintage: Poet Tempo	Invoice: C05394
Karma Reading in: 222591	Karma reading out: 730

Invoice to:
Gabriela Anaya del Alma
7443 Draper Street
La Jolla, CA 92121

Concern 51 Correction	Inspect and replace Nirmanakaya	Operation Tech 1 106
Comment Parts	Part # Dharma E432 Heartstream assembly Dharma F8CZ Tummo fan and switch Dharma 8K621A Voice filter replaced	Quantity 1 1 1
Type C	Tech 106: Jampa Dorje	

Date: 10/06/06

SUMMARY: All parts and service are under warranty.
A 30 day test run is proposed with no obligation.

Restoration authorization and depository receipt
(AB 409 amending civil code)

X ☐

From: Gabriela Anaya del Alma
To: Rychard Artaud
Sent: Saturday, October 07, 2006 12:32 PM
Subject: Restoration

Dear Jampa

I love so many of the ideas you have had for Bouvard's restoration! And I hope he is indeed as pleasantly attuned as you assure. But I may yet need to undo some of your magic, and invoke some sexual spells of my own. Again, I fear that Boo has become too much of a clockwork chocolate to inspire my passions.

And perhaps it is just as well that Rychard is not quite ready, even if well on the way to reform. A harem is a daunting responsibility. And as you know, it is difficult for me to labor thus, even on weekends, since I have almost zero time alone, now that Jacques has returned from his walkabout. I may well murder him, simply for daring to intrude his eyes into my creative space.

Also, I have two shows this weekend where my work is on display, and I will be away for hours, today and tomorrow, even though I would rather go buy some new tap pants and a red wig.

Love,

Gabriela

Yes, I quite expected you would make adjustments to my android, and reprogram him to your specifications. Remember that this model of android does dream of sheep, and that the key to their performing the moves of love is that they understand their meaning. Well, Bouvard is yours, as soon as you sign the release. You needn't use blood; ink is fine, or blue lipstick.

Dance on,

Jampa

Dear Jampa,

I'm off to an art opening. I have to think over everything. I appreciate what you've done with my boys. But will I miss their fire?

Until tomorrow,

Gabriela Anaya del Alma

181

From: Jampa Dorje
To: Gabriela Anaya del Alma
Sent: Sunday, October 08, 2006 7:45 PM
Subject: Bouvard's boilers

Miss Gabriela,

ssssssssssssssssssssssssssssssssssssssssssssssssssssssssssssssssssssssssssssssssssssssssss
ssssssssssssssssssssssssssssssssssssssssssssssssssssssssssssssssssssssssssssssssssssssssss
ssssssssssssssssssssssssssssssssssssssssssssssssssssssssssssssssssssssssssssssssssssssssss
sssssssssssssssssssssssssssssssssssssssssssssssssss

These esses represent the steam escaping from Bouvard's boilers. I am thankful as well. This could have been a disaster. Things were at feverish pitch when your two boys, as you call them, came to me for help. The ramifications of Bouvard's and Rychard's karma had caught up with them. It's a quaint idea that an old monk could make a few adjustments and things would be like new. Yes, I replaced the basic assembly of Bouvard's mind-view. In other words, I turned him around with a few pithy instructions, but the basic material of his nature remains unchanged, including, as you may be happy to hear, the fire.

The fire of Bouvard is different than the fire of Rychard. This is due to their upbringing and education. Bouvard, although a man of the 21st century, still has the manners of a 19th century gentleman at heart. Rychard will always be a brute. Both, of course are members of the NovaNaieve Movement, but they are distinctly different animals.

I know that Bouvard will seem a bit rigid and clock-like at first. This is to be expected. This is Bouvard. Give him a chance. The potentiation to go beyond old boundaries is much greater now. This Bouvard will be the same Bouvard you loved before, but now he will be warmer, closer, more caring, more, dare I say it, committed. I am positive you will be fully satisfied. Take your time;

relax; turn the dials; rev him up. You know the drill: start with a walk, move to a trot, proceed to canter, then reign him in. Don't run him full out right at first. I don't want to get technical here, but during this early critical period excitatory transmission and plasticity on the star pyramid layer must remain unaltered, and an accelerated time course for control will most likely deprive the hemispheric pairs of their initial pairing protocols, and this could produce a flame-out as you approach absolute fusion, if you understand my drift, and I'm sure you do.

Anyway, he's yours with my blessing, and with your consent. Stay in touch.

Yours,

Jampa

From: Gabriela Anaya del Alma
To: Jampa Dorje
Sent: Thursday, October 12, 2006 9:39 AM
Subject: Fever

Dear Jampa,

I have been ill, and forced to rely on the attentions of Jacques, who has delighted in my fever. Yesterday afternoon I felt better, and insisted he go visit again that old woman in the desert. I don't know when he is coming back.

All last night I dreamt fingers through my hair, and soft whispers. I dreamt I was at peace, and that there was nothing left to imagine. I dreamt of the monk in his cloister; the poet in his mine; the conqueror wandering the waste; the lover fumbling at the gate.

I awoke, signed the release, then found, slipped under my door, this poem from Bouvard:

AT DAWN

I take endless journeys in russet light,
moving through a landscape of love, again,
without ever finding the wind's source.

I am surrounded by a miracle of clouds.
My memory is as heavy as a clear winter,
and my heart is an azure tumult.

Oh Jampa, a new and yet familiar fever takes me over.

A Brief Chronology

1941   Rychard Artaud born in Berkeley, California.

1942   Harvey Goldner born in Tennessee.

1944   Jampa Dorje (né Jubal Dolan) born in Oakland, California.

1946   Bouvard Pécuchet born in Oakland, California.

1951   Jacques Bâtard born in Brussels, Belgium, where his father is professor of mathematics at the Free University of Brussels.

1954   Bouvard meets Jampa (Jubal), at school in Oakland.

1961   Bouvard is committed, for three months, to Napa State Mental Hospital, Imola, California.

1962   Jacques' mother dies. Father moves to the U.S., to take up professorship at the University of Texas, Austin.

1962   Rychard enrolls at the University of California, Berkeley.

1963   Gabriela Anaya del Alma born in Mexico City.

1963   Bouvard leaves home, aiming to reach New York City.

1963   Bouvard sentenced, for one year term, to juvenile detention in Waco, Texas.

1964   Jacques sentenced, for one year term, to same juvenile detention center in Waco, Texas.

1964   Bouvard released. Returns to Oakland, and enrolls in Merrit College.

1965   Berkeley Poetry Conference. Bouvard and Jampa (Jubal) attend, and meet Rychard Artaud.

1965   Jacques released, and returns to Austin, Texas.

1966   Jampa (Jubal) moves to Alaska.

1967   Rychard joins State Farm Insurance, in Oakland, California.

1968   Jampa (Jubal) enrolls in the University of Alaska.

1969	Jacques enrolls in University of Texas at Austin.
1969	Gabriela moves to Fort Worth, Texas.
1971	Jacques continues his studies at the Free University of Brussels, Belgium.
1972	Bouvard travels through New Mexico, then on to Mexico and Central America.
1975	Jacques' first trip to the Congo.
1975	Jampa (Jubal) founds Four Winds Bookstore in Ellensburg, Washington.
1978	Jacques pursues graduate studies in linguistics at Harvard University.
1977	Bouvard begins work as tree planter in Ellensburg, Washington.
1980	Rychard begins in earnest his vocation as an independent publisher.
1983	Gabriela employed as dancer, in New Orleans, Louisiana.
1987	Gabriela enrolls in beauty school, in Fort Worth, Texas.
1989	Jampa (Jubal) sells bookstore, enters Buddhist retreat.
1990	Jacques and Bouvard begin their three year Odyssey, up and down the West Coast, then on through Arizona, New Mexico, and Texas. Jacques meets Harvey Goldner in Seattle, Washington, and Rychard in Oakland, California.
1993	Jacques and Bouvard escape from the Davidian Compound, Waco, Texas.
1993	Bouvard's pilgrimmage to Tibet. Jacques' second trip to the Congo.
1998	Rychard cares for his elderly parents, in Santa Rosa, California.
1998	Gabriela moves to San Diego.
1999	Jacques moves to San Diego.
2002	Jacques meets Gabriela.
2006	Mills College Poetry Conference. Gabriela meets Rychard, Bouvard, and Harvey Goldner.